MW00437844

# RETURN TO THE WILDERNESS

## FRONTIER HEARTS
### BOOK FOUR

## ANDREA BYRD

WILD HEART
BOOKS

Copyright © 2024 by Andrea Byrd

All rights reserved. No portion of this book may be reproduced or transmitted in any form or by any means - photocopied, shared electronically, scanned, stored in a retrieval system, or other - without the express permission of the publisher. Exceptions will be made for brief quotations used in critical reviews or articles promoting this work.

The characters and events in this fictional work are the product of the author's imagination. Any resemblance to actual people, living or dead, is coincidental.

Unless otherwise indicated, all Scripture quotations are taken from the Holy Bible, Kings James Version.

ISBN-13: 978-1-963212-07-5

# CHAPTER 1

*M*uireall's hands flew to her mouth, stifling the scream that came as a scraggly man leapt from within the branches of a red maple as her sister passed. Green leaves rustled as he landed upon her sister's lean form, his momentum toppling them both to the ground. Margaret scrambled out from under him, but he grabbed her ankles and yanked her back. Meanwhile, tears streamed down Muireall's face, for she knew no matter how hard she attempted to move, she was bound in place.

Muireall bolted upright, but darkness enveloped her. She swiped at the tears on her face and gasped for breath. The room seemed as devoid of air as it was of light. Clambering to the head of her cot, she located the

1

candle on the bedside table and fumbled to light it. Finally, a small flame broke through the inky black, and her breathing began to slow. 'Twas only a dream. The same dream that had plagued her every night for two weeks—but still, only a dream.

Why was she afflicted with these nightmares now, nearly four years after she and her sister were attacked in their own home? Because something was terribly wrong. A shiver ran through Muireall.

Nay. She shook her head and moved to start a fire in the hearth, as if the movement could shake the trepidation from her bones. Margaret was safe, living in the home their father had built near the Green River. A tear slipped down her cheek. How could she know that for sure?

Muireall had not received a single word from Margaret in the time since her sister returned home. There was no mail service on the frontier, after all. One rarely even had visitors. With this knowledge, Muireall had been forced to assume Margaret and her husband had made it safely home, where they started their family. And she had lived peacefully with that assumption...until the nightmares came. Dread swirled in her stomach.

Once Muireall had coaxed the flames to life and hung a kettle of water over the fire, she wrapped herself in a wool shawl and threw open the door. A cold breeze greeted her, the chill of night not yet having been pushed out by the sun's warmth. Though the world outside was a blur, a smudge of pink on the horizon revealed that soon, all would be bathed in light. Hopefully, it would edge the gloominess out of her soul.

Still, there was a portion of Muireall that longed to return to her sister's side, to ensure that all was well with her only remaining relation. A frown tugged the edges of her mouth downward. She could never do that. Traveling back into the wilderness would mean enlisting the aid of someone who could see more than five inches in front of their own face. And she could never let anyone know her secret. Margaret was not even aware of her blemish. Nay, Muireall's mither had made it clear that should anyone find out, it would ruin her chances at marriage.

As it was, her beauty and skill with a needle should result in a match. At least, that was what Ma had iterated time and time again. Yet here she was at twenty-one years of age, with not a single prospect. Of course, she kept mostly to herself, sewing and caring for Petunia. It was much easier to keep her distance from strangers. Less chance of revealing her secret. But it was a lonely existence.

With that thought, Muireall closed the door against the chilly March morning and glanced toward the bed where Petunia continued to slumber. Her chest squeezed as she conjured an image of the elderly woman's bony features. When she and her sister had arrived at the fort, Petunia had taken Muireall under her wing and helped her find some worth in her abilities, particularly those involving needle and thread, outside of marriage. Not only had she shared her home, but under her tutelage, Muireall had bloomed.

Over the past winter, though, Petunia's health had declined. Now it was she that needed Muireall. No matter how pressing the sensation that her sister was in danger, she could never leave the person to whom she owed so much.

~

*J*ohn passed the bounds of the fort and slipped over to the nearest oak. There, he leaned against the trunk with arms crossed and hat pulled low over his face while he waited for Hodges and Rollinson. Why did it have to be those two vermin from his past who held the key to finding his father? The men were acquaintances from what seemed a lifetime ago. Worthless rabble-rousers who enjoyed their women, liquor, and thievery. John thought he had left that life behind him when he came west. But here it was, swaggering toward him in the form of a lanky blonde and a stocky redhead.

"Jude Browne. You sure are a sight for sore eyes." Hodges's gaze landed on the leather eyepatch covering John's useless right eye before he snickered at Rollinson, the taller of the two men. John's body tensed at the use of his given name, and his fingers dug into his arms through his shirtsleeves. He forced them to relax and lifted a smile to the newcomers. He needed them on his side, for now.

"Could say the same of the two of you."

Rollinson released a steely laugh that could curdle blood. His blue eyes narrowed on John. "I hear people around here call you by John."

"Yes." John tried to keep the bite from his voice, but his jaw clenched. Rollinson had the power to bring the new life he had built crashing down around him. Only, he would have to bring himself down in the process. But a man like him might believe he was immune, so John had better tread lightly. "It is simpler for folk around here." He gave a one-shoulder shrug.

Rollinson eyed him a moment longer before he spat into the greening grass of the coming spring. "What do you want, Jude?"

Thankful the man preferred to cut to the chase, John breathed a sigh of relief. If he could resolve this business and retreat to his cabin before anyone ventured by, perhaps his façade would remain intact. "I need a map to Pitman Station."

"Plan on going on a trip?" Hodges raised bushy red eyebrows over beady brown eyes.

"I have business there."

Hodges and Rollinson exchanged conspiratorial glances, and though John kept his expression blank, his insides began to crawl. Perhaps this had not been his brightest idea, involving these two. But despite all his faults, Rollinson was a gifted cartographer. Why the man had taken to carousing instead of pursuing the use of his gift, John would never know. But he supposed everyone had skeletons from their past. He certainly had his own, and this conversation was living, breathing proof. Still, with a map of Rollinson's creation in John's hand, he could not go astray as he continued his hunt for his father. As long as it was accurate and Rollinson did not attempt to purposefully deceive him. Jude shifted, sizing up the man he once worked alongside.

"What is in it for us?"

Jude was prepared for Rollinson's question. He withdrew a hefty bag of coins from his pocket and tossed it in the air before catching it again and stuffing it back into place. "I will pay a handsome sum." Perhaps the money would be incentive to keep Rollinson honest in his map-making.

He would not need much on the frontier, anyway. Only what supplies he could carry. He had heard Pitman Station was only a week's journey by foot, so he did not even intend to buy a horse. The less to tend to, the better. No ties, nothing to weigh him down or trip him up, as he searched for the man who had left his mother before John was ever born. Maybe then he would know who he truly was.

Rollinson's lips tipped up. "I will have it for you in two days' time."

"Good." This time, a genuine smile spread across John's lips. He pushed himself from the tree and gave a tip of his hat. After six years of waiting and searching, finally, he had a substantial lead...and a way to track it down.

~

*M*uireall covered her mouth as she stifled a yawn.

"Still having nightmares?" Concern laced Betty Davidson's voice. Her best friend sat at the table with her, sipping a cup of tea. Her frizzy brown waves were tucked into a knot at her nape, and the worry in her equally brown eyes matched her voice.

"Aye." Muireall glanced toward the bed to ensure that Petunia still slumbered, the elderly woman having laid back down after a bit of porridge and an hour spent sewing. Thankfully, she slept soundly. Though Petunia had been a wise and trusted confidante over the past few years, Muireall did not wish to burden her with her troubles, not with the precarious state of her health.

The scraping of Betty's chair against the floor drew her attention back to her friend. "Come along. Let us take a walk. 'Tis a bright, beautiful day—if a bit chilly." Betty took her elbow and coaxed her toward the open door.

Muireall smiled. After her own health scare the autumn after they arrived at the fort, Betty had roped her into taking daily constitutionals. And despite her aversion to the outdoors, Muireall had to admit, the fresh air and sunshine always brightened her spirits. It was also thanks to her friend that she and Petunia worked with their door propped open as often as not.

Truly, Muireall enjoyed their time outside on days such as this. A cool breeze ruffled her hair while the sun warmed her cheeks. Only, life was safer in her and Petunia's little cabin. She knew the location of each item and usually, all she needed was within her reach. There was no risk of her blundering in an unfamiliar environment and revealing her secret.

"It still seems strange that the nightmares would come now, years after you were attacked." Betty led her out onto the worn path that stretched in front of the row of matching cabins.

"I know." Trauma was the most logical explanation, though. The only other explanation was that the dreams were an omen. Muireall shivered.

"Have you considered going to your sister?"

Muireall's gaze snapped to her blurry friend. Betty did not beat around the bush. "Oh, I could never leave Petunia. Her health is too unstable these days. She needs me." The first person who ever had. Normally, she was the one in need. And the scales would tip back to their normal balance should she traipse into the wilderness.

"True." Betty paused. "But if you are honest with yourself, if you had no obligations here, would you go?"

Muireall tipped her chin as she considered. She would be sorely tempted. But there was still the issue of her eyesight and her need for a guide. There was simply no way such a trip would ever be possible. No matter how her stomach tightened with concern for her sister.

But what if her nightmares truly meant something deeper? Would her sister not come for her? After all, her sister had married a stranger, left her home, and uprooted her entire life for Muireall's safety only four years prior. She had made the journey and nearly lost her new husband in the process.

Margaret had always been the stronger of the two of them.

"I would love to be able to go to her, to ensure her safety. But 'tis not that simple." Muireall gave a shrug.

Betty sighed. "Yes. I only hate to see you sufferin' so." She squeezed Muireall's arm. "I will pray that you are able to find some peace."

"I appreciate it."

Silence fell over them as they soaked in the sun's rays. But it only lasted so long as it took them to reach the end of the row of cabins. No sooner than they turned around and Betty gasped. Muireall turned wide eyes upon her.

"Did you hear? Mrs. Cooper is expecting!" With her own womb barren, Betty took even greater pleasure than most in the arrival of young ones in Harrodstown.

"Oh, how wonderful." Without a doubt, Muireall would find herself sewing a gown for the bairn, whether on commission or simply as a gift to the new parents.

A figure approached down the path, and Muireall

sidled closer to Betty. She scrutinized the newcomer, but it was no use. The man wore a hat and dressed in dark clothing, just as most of the men in the area did. She prayed that Betty would recognize the neighbor and greet them so that she might be able to do so without blunder. The man kept his head down, but as he neared, he gave them a quick glance and nod. Was he wearing an eyepatch?

"Good afternoon, Mr. Browne." Betty waved cheerfully. But the man continued marching down the path, past them, his head bent as though he was on an important mission. "Such a strange man," her friend added, without a hint of judgement.

"Mhmm." Muireall murmured her agreement as she reluctantly moved her attention from his retreating form.

Betty prattled on about the gorgeous weather with which they had been blessed and how planting would soon begin, but Muireall found it difficult to focus on her words. Instead, she worked to tamp down the strange sensation that swirled in her middle.

Finally, she and Betty had made their way back to the cabin. Maybe all would be better once she put needle to cloth. There was such a soothing rhythm to sewing.

As soon as the two stepped into the dim cabin, Muireall's heart dropped. Something was amiss. Eerie silence filled the room and threatened to drown her in its wake. Immediately, she went to Petunia's side. Her hand trembled as she placed it upon the elderly woman's chest. There was no rise and fall.

"No!" The word came out as a garbled sob as she doubled over upon herself.

"Oh, honey." Betty was by her side in an instant, her arm around her shoulder, supporting her.

Murieall's only companion in life was gone. And suddenly, the tables had shifted.

# CHAPTER 2

*MARCH 20, 1784*

*M*uireall stared at the fresh mound of dirt before her but could not bring herself to move. Of those who attended Petunia's funeral, only the Reverend Patterson and Betty remained. Even those who had shoveled the dirt over the pine box had retreated to their other duties. Still, Muireall's feet remained anchored to the ground.

Reverend Patterson stepped toward her, drawing her attention from the blurry brown mass. His touch was light on her elbow. "If you need anything, do not hesitate to let me know." His pale blue eyes were kind, his mouth pressed into an empathetic line.

Muireall sighed before she nodded in response. "Thank ye." Then he was gone as well.

She swept her gaze back to the dirt. The problem

was, she did not have an inkling as to what she needed at this point. Her constant companion of the past four years was gone. No longer would she hear the gentle creak of the wooden rocker or the out-of-rhythm tug of thread through fabric as the two sewed together, each focused on their individual projects while working together in quiet harmony.

Betty would remain a faithful friend and beacon of light in this time of darkness, though. She had already proven such over the last couple of days. And Muireall could easily continue to provide for herself with her prosperous sewing and mending business. But the nightmares did not die with Petunia. And each day, it seemed, the weight of guilt pulled heavier as a burdensome yoke about her neck. Dread grew like a black vine within her middle and threatened to consume her if she did not go to her sister. Muireall closed her eyes and pressed back tears.

No longer did she have the excuse of Petunia's care to hide behind. And yet, leaving the fort seemed an insurmountable task.

"She would want you to move on." Betty's quiet voice broke into her thoughts.

Muireall nodded again as she stifled a sob. Of course, Petunia would want her to move on. Though she hid it behind the selfless excuse of protecting Petunia's health, perhaps that was why she had never disclosed the occurrence of her unsettling dreams to her companion. To hide behind her own cowardice.

She could almost hear Petunia's raspy voice urging her, "Go with the Lord's calling, my child."

Betty gave her arm a reassuring squeeze.

Muireall offered her the smallest of smiles and patted her friend's hand where it rested on her arm. "Ye go on. I would like a moment alone."

"Are you sure?"

"Aye. I will return directly."

Betty gave her one last lingering look, a frown set on her face as though she were not quite convinced, before she turned and headed up the hill to the fort.

After she watched her friend's retreating back, Muireall faced the grave. With no audience, she knelt to the ground and placed her hand on the cool dirt. "Ye would want me to go to me sister, would ye not?" She asked the question, though she knew there would be no answer. But at that moment, the clouds parted overhead, and a bright ray of warm sunshine broke through the chill of the day, settling over her.

Muireall turned to the sky and spoke to her heavenly Father. "How come Margaret could follow Yer will, but I cannae?" Her heart twisted at the thought, and she bit her lip.

Then, with a deep sigh, she rose from the ground. Perhaps her sister was simply made of stronger stuff than she. Slowly, she trudged up the hill. A few men stood talking under a tall oak several yards away, but she paid them no mind. Just placed one foot in front of the other. Until two words snagged her attention. "One map to Pitman Station."

Muireall froze. Pitman Station? That station was within a day's travel of home. In fact, she, her sister, and her sister's husband had stayed there on the first night of their journey to the fort. She moved closer while staying behind the cover of the tree.

Another voice replied in a clipped tone, followed by the jingle of coins. "This shall make travel easier. Thank you."

Was someone traveling to the station? If someone was already planning to make the journey, mayhap she could tag along without revealing her secret. And though she might not be able to see worth a shilling, from there, she should be able to make her way home. Crossing the Green River would be her greatest obstacle.

"I would say it should," the first voice replied. "You never did say what your business was there, though."

So the person did have business at Pitman Station as well as being in possession of a map to the destination. Was this her sign? Muireall squeezed her eyes shut while her heart beat wildly. *Is this Ye, Lord? Do Ye truly wish to for me to go to Margaret?* Giddiness bubbled in her heart when she considered seeing her sister's face and propelled her forward, past all fear and hesitation.

"Pitman Station?" Suddenly, she was around the tree and staring at three men. The indistinct forms of a tall blonde and a short, stocky redhead stood a few feet away while a third man whirled to face her. Disturbingly close, she was met with one deep-brown eye set in a scarred face and another hidden behind a leather eyepatch. Muireall's mouth drifted open.

~

*B*lue eyes peered up at John from a pale, porcelain face. A face that he recognized but could not place. When he failed to answer, the woman's gaze darted between him and the other men. "Are ye goin' there? To Pitman Station?" She looked back at him, her voice breathless.

Muireall, that was her name. Betty's friend and a talent with a needle. What did she want with Pitman Station? While he did not wish to involve her, he could not lie. He swallowed. "Yes."

Her lips parted, then pressed together as if she were at war with herself. "Can...can I come with ye?"

It was as though John had been punched in the stomach.

"We can take you there, honey," Rollinson offered from behind him, his voice laced with deceptive sweetness.

"No." John's forceful protest left his lips, and he had stepped between Rollinson and Muireall before he even realized what he was doing. A pucker formed between her dark brows.

He had to protect this woman from Hodges and

Rollinson. He could not consciously allow her to be ruined by their dishonest charms. But was he any better, to lead her into the wilderness alone? Who would ever believe that a one-eyed rogue such as he would leave her reputation intact? Just as it had been for his mother, her good name would be shattered forever. So where did that leave them? "I mean to say... I will take you." He heaved in a deep breath. "If we are married." It was the only solution.

Muireall's eyes went as wide as saucers. She opened her mouth to speak, but he held up a hand to stop her. No more should be discussed in front of Hodges and Rollinson. Plus, she needed an opportunity to consider her answer. No woman should have to be shackled to him as a wife, but it definitely should not be done on a whim. "I know where your cabin is. May I come discuss this with you further when my business here is complete?"

Muireall nodded slowly before she turned and headed up the hillside to the fort, alone. Heat prickled up the back of his neck. What had he done?

~

*M*uireall paced the tiny cabin. Three steps one way, three back in the other direction. Repeat. Marriage? How could she have gotten herself into such a predicament? What had possessed her to ask a random stranger to escort her to Pitman

Station? Of course, she could not travel alone with a man. Oh, the kind of loose woman people would have thought her to be upon arrival.

Muireall turned and dropped onto the bed. The bed where Petunia had died. Fresh tears filled her eyes, and she pressed the palms of her hands against them. That was why she asked. She could not stay here in this cabin filled with the stench of loss. The minute room had turned into a massive void of loneliness. Now, nothing tied her to the fort besides her sewing work and her friendship with Betty. And the desire to go to her sister pulled on her stronger than ever, with such a power that it could not be ignored. So when she had heard Pitman Station mentioned, she had leapt at the opportunity.

*Lord, what have I done? Was this Yer will, or did I act in haste an' ruin everythin'?*

She sighed. Despite the man's roguish appearance and the fact she knew nothing about him, this was an answer to another prayer. One she had not prayed in some time. To find a husband. With her sewing, she had a purpose outside of keeping her secret and waiting for the right man to come along. But if she left the fort, the opportunity to marry might never come again.

Muireall stood and resumed her pacing. Moments later, a knock sounded on the door, and her heart leapt into double time. She paused before opening it. The man with the eyepatch stepped into her cabin and moved into what little open space there was. If possible, the room shrunk in size. She backed toward the small table beside the bed and clasped her hands onto it as though it could anchor her.

Her visitor removed his hat and held it in his hands. "I...I did not mean to be presumptuous back there. I only wish to protect your reputation if we are to travel together."

Muireall nodded. The man's voice was deep, with a slight rasp. But somehow, it soothed her swirling insides. "I understand. An' I did not wish to place ye in a precarious situation. I can find other arrangements if need be." The man deserved a chance to change his mind now that there was no audience. After all, he would never want to marry her if he knew the truth— that she was defective.

But where would that leave her? The other men had offered to take her to Pitman Station, but that would mean she would be traveling alone with two men instead of one. And simply the thought of those two twisted her stomach and made her want to run in the other direction. Muireall was not sure why, as she had not even been able to see them clearly. But a trepidation stirred deep within.

Should she be afraid of this man too? His profile was certainly rough enough. Muireall ventured a step closer, propelled by a desire to glimpse his face again in detail.

The man let out a sigh and rapped his knuckles on the table beside him, as though he had decided. "Other arrangements are not necessary. I only want you to be comfortable with your decision, Muireall."

Her lips parted "How do ye know me name?"

His shoulder lifted. "I have seen you with Betty and heard your name spoken about the fort. You liv—lived with Petunia and are excellent with a needle and thread."

Muireall smiled. After all this time, her mither's plan seemed to have come to fruition. At least, in a sense. But what did she know about him?

She took another step closer, but his features were still blurred, his gaze cast toward the floor. Did he avoid her regard for a reason? "What is yer name?"

His attention moved to her. "John Browne."

Muireall nodded, but the corners of her mouth pulled downward. While it was imperative knowledge should she marry this man, it told her nothing of who he truly was. "Do ye have a trade?"

John hesitated. Was that a frown? "I mostly trap and hunt. I try to make myself useful where I can."

Honorable enough, she supposed. "And what is your business at Pitman Station?"

"I...I am looking for someone. And you? What makes a young woman such as yourself wish to travel into the wilderness to a remote station?"

"I am lookin' for someone as well. Me sister. She lives near there. An', well...she needs me." She could not tell him more than that. He might believe her to be crazed.

John nodded. "I understand. I will be glad to take you as long as we marry before we set out. You can determine the nature of our marriage if you wish, whether it be in name alone or...more. But I cannot be the cause of your ruin." He stepped closer, and even she could tell there was an intensity to his gaze as it met hers. He took her hand in his and pressed it. "Also I urge you not to allow Rollinson and Hodges to be your escort. Even if you will not have me."

Muireall's mouth dropped open as heat flared up her neck and into her face. Her breath became shallow. A fierce protectiveness emanated from the man before her, and it drew her, like a moth to the flame. She dipped her chin in a nod. "I will have ye. As me husband."

*Lord, please dinnae let me be burned.*

# CHAPTER 3

*MARCH 21, 1784*

*a* gust of wind brought a small tree branch crashing to the ground near John's feet as he latched the corral gate behind the mare. The aged animal snorted but continued to graze. He shivered against the cold rain that blew against his face and pushed his hat lower on his head. While the weather may not be cooperating with his and Muireall's plans for travel, at least that was one task completed. With most of his funds depleted, the old horse was all he could afford. But his wife would not have to walk the distance to the station.

His middle tightened. Within the next few days, he would be a married man. Though he had never wished to marry, John had yet to come up with a satisfactory alternative to their situation. And he would do the best he could by his wife. Muireall's face flashed into his mind, with her porcelain skin and hesitant smile, and he set his feet in the direction of her cabin. He crossed the fort and followed the path to the last cabin on the right.

John knocked on the wooden door and waited.

Within moments, Muireall appeared before him. "John. Good afternoon. Come in out of the rain." She stepped aside and motioned him in. The corners of her mouth were tipped up, but she busied herself with the kettle hanging over the fire. "Care for a cup o' tea?"

"Oh. No, thank you. I cannot stay long. I only wanted to let you know that I have acquired a horse to aid in our travel. Her name is Sugar, and though she is fifteen years old, she seems to have a level head."

"Wonderful." Muireall kept her gaze averted and focused on pouring herself a cup of tea. "Do ye know when we might leave?"

John shifted. Was she regretting her decision? "If the weather turns for the better, I do not see why we could not leave in a couple of days. Do you believe you could be ready by then?" He watched and waited, gauging her reaction.

Muireall nodded and looked to him, her cup of tea nestled between her hands. "Aye. I can be ready anytime. An'...we will be married then, before we leave?"

He swallowed. The one task he had avoided thus far. "Yes. I will speak with Reverend Patterson tomorrow." Now John found himself avoiding her gaze. He rubbed at a crack in the top of the straight-back chair next to the door. "You are sure of your decision?" He had to ask.

"Aye." Muireall's response came quick and sure and drew his attention back to her. Her slender chin tipped upward as she looked at him square on. It stole John's breath. Here this woman stood, unwavering and unafraid to tie herself to him. Without knowing his past and despite the repellant nature of his face, she stood firm. Her dedication to her sister must be profound. It could be the only explanation. Still, a strange sensation crawled across the top of his shoulders.

John cleared his throat. "Then I will speak with the reverend tomorrow and let you know what he says."

"Thank ye." Her voice softened then, and he was unprepared for the way it affected him.

It was time for him to retreat to his own tiny cabin nestled in the woods outside the fort. He gave a polite nod. "Have a good night, Muireall." His tone rasped as he spoke.

As soon as she had returned the salutation, he ducked through the door and out into the cool rain. Wind gusseted his body, but he plowed down the path toward the open gate. Why had he not been clearer on the terms of their marriage? Demanded that, without a shadow of a doubt, it be in name only?

*MARCH 23, 1784*

uireall pushed the needle through the fabric and pulled it out through the back, expecting at any moment that a shadow would fall over her. Outside, water dripped from the roof of the cabin into the puddles below, but sun streamed in through the open door. The rain had finally come to an end, and bright rays of light worked to push out the remaining clouds. That meant she would be married and set on a different path the next day. She did not need John to stop by and advise her so for he had already disclosed as much. When he spoke with Reverend Patterson the day before, it was agreed upon that as soon as the weather broke, he and Muireall would be married the next morning and set out directly after. Butterflies took flight in her middle as she considered embarking on the new adventure, and she refocused her attention on the steady rhythm of her sewing. In and out she drew the thread, in and out.

Just when she had lost herself in the peace of it, the shadow came. A rapid knock sounded on the doorframe, and her spine went straight as she whipped toward the sound. Rather than her betrothed, Betty stood in the doorway. Her ever-present smile was in place, and she carried a large basket filled with what appeared to be an assortment of goods.

Muireall's mouth twisted to the side, and she raised a brow at her friend. "What have ye been up to?"

As Muireall deposited her project in her sewing basket, Betty set the basket on the table. "I know you did not want to announce that you were leaving because you did not wish everyone to come knocking on your door. But I know how much you mean to everyone here, and I wanted you to know what an impact you have made. So I made the rounds on your behalf. And this is the outpouring of love shown by your neighbors." Betty turned and beamed at her, her chest puffed with pride.

Muireall's mouth fell open as she looked from her companion to the contents of the basket. "This is for me?" She fingered the edge of a quilt that poked out from the plethora of gifts. While the fabric was well-worn, it meant that it had kept someone warm on many occasions and had been proffered out of love, not because it was superfluous.

"Yes. You will be deeply missed." Betty gave her arm a squeeze.

Tears welled in Muireall's eyes. Though the people of Harrodstown had kept her in steady work with need of her skills, she had never stopped to consider what an affect her presence had on the community. And yet, piled before her was a deluge of adoration and respect. It did not matter that she had remained a recluse outside of her daily constitutionals with Betty. Still, these people gave that which they did not have to give.

It was time for her to exhibit such selflessness, to step from what was comfortable into that which would stretch her capacities. She glanced around and her stomach dropped. Despite several days of warning, she had barely begun to pack. Each time she had made an attempt, fear that she might need one item or another had crept in. The overwhelming desire to keep all as it had been had paralyzed her.

Betty's gasp at her side revealed that she had followed Muireall's gaze...and her thinking. "You have yet to begin packing? Are you having second thoughts? Have you changed your mind?"

"Nay. Nay." Muireall's protest came too quickly and adamantly. Betty scrutinized her, and it was clear her friend saw straight through to her heart. Her shoulders sagged, and she sighed as she flopped into the chair beside the table. "Well...how well do ye know Mr. Browne? Truly?"

Betty took the other of the two straight-back chairs that sat at the square table in the corner. She scooted close and took Muireall's hands into hers. "I only know that when my husband was down with broken leg, he saw to it that we had meat every night. I tried to wave him off and explain that we could easily live off of bread and fresh vegetables. But he would not have it."

"Ye do make the best bread." Muireall chuckled.

"See?" Betty flashed a grin before she continued. "He also takes food and wares to Widow Kline each day. She told me once when I went to visit her."

Muireall glanced toward the door, her mind reeling. Widow Kline was a blind woman who kept a homestead a couple miles from the fort. She and her husband had been some of the first to settle the area, and even after he passed and her eyes failed her, she refused to leave the place she called home. If John provided for her, would that mean he would be amenable to providing for a woman who was only half blind? But a spirited, elderly widow was such a different story. Her name was known all around, and Muireall doubted Mr. Browne was the only one tending to her needs.

Muireall, on the other hand, was just broken but without the widow's stalwart reputation.

"Muireall, you know if I did not believe him to be an honorable man, I would tell you."

She had to smile then. Betty was not one to mince words or withhold the truth. "Aye. Ye would."

"Do we have some packing to do, then?"

"Aye." The tension eased from Muireall's shoulders as Betty slapped her knees and rose to her feet. Together they took on the challenge of packing her belongings as well as the new supplies.

After folding her clothing and tucking them into a carpetbag, Muireall turned to the basket atop her table. She frowned as she lifted a bag of dried beans. "Should John an' I have separate packs of food stores, or should they be combined?"

Betty came up behind her. "Well, I supposed it would make more sense to combine all you can."

A form appeared in the doorway, and Muireall's heart seemed to stutter and skip a beat as she laid eyes upon her soon-to-be-husband. "John. I suppose ye can assist with our dilemma."

He withdrew his hat as he stepped into the room. He gave a nod to Betty and turned his attention to Muireall. "How can I help?"

"We have been given many generous gifts, an' I wondered about the best way to pack them. I know my personal items will be stowed separately, but what of these food stores? Should our wares not be combined?"

John nodded as he peered into the basket. "That would be advisable." Then he glanced between the two women. "All of this is for us?" He seemed as bewildered as Muireall had been, and it warmed her to see.

"It is," Betty declared from behind them, a smile in her voice.

"I will take all of the food stores with me, then, if I may borrow this basket to transport them. I...I only came to let you know that we will be married the morning after next." With his arms atop the basket, he seemed hesitant to look Muireall's way. He turned his head only slightly in her direction.

She placed a hand on his arm to set him at ease. "Verra well."

Finally, John turned and lifted the corners of his

mouth, at least for her sake. "Well, I will leave you to your preparations. Do you need anything?"

When their eyes met, Muireall's mouth went dry. The concern that was reflected in her betrothed's gaze went well beyond if she was in need of thread or beans or some other item. The man before her cared, and cared deeply, regarding her welfare.

"I am quite well." She breathed out the reply. In that moment, she had no doubt that John's intentions were benevolent and that he would see to her every need on the trail. Every need that she disclosed to him, that was.

~

This could not be how most men spent the afternoon before their wedding. "Now pull the hammer back," John instructed Muireall from where he hovered precariously close to her shoulder. When his wife-to-be had done as he advised, he added, "Look down the barrel to your target and squeeze the trigger when you are ready."

Their chosen target was the knot on a large oak tree behind Widow Kline's cabin. The elderly woman was more than glad to sit on her back porch and act as a chaperone of sorts while John attempted to acclimate Muireall to shooting his pistol away from the general populace. As he had run through his mental list of the preparations that needed to be made, ensuring that his wife could defend herself on the Kentucky frontier was one task that had slipped through the cracks. Now, she stood before him taking an inordinate amount of time to aim. Finally, the pistol fired.

"Didn't hit it, did she?" Widow Kline called from her rocking chair. The rhythmic creak of wood upon wood never faltered.

"Nope." How had the blind woman known that Muireall had not even touched the tree? John gentled his voice before he spoke again. "That is perfectly normal for your first attempt. Now, this time, is there one eye that seems stronger than the other?"

Muireall swallowed and glanced away. In someone like Hodges, it would have been a tell that he was lying. From this slender woman, though, it surely meant she was uncomfortable discussing such matters with him. In fact, it was likely a detail she had never considered. "When you are writing or sewing, do you ever close one eye to see better?"

Muireall seemed to think it over. "Maybe me left."

"Good. So, this time, try closing your left eye when you shoot."

After a timid nod of her head, she followed his instructions again, paying special attention to each detail. He took a step back and allowed her some space. Still, her shot went wide, rustling through some leaves on the tree next to her target. Jude's brows furrowed.

"Missed again," called the leathery voice from behind them. Muireall's shoulders slumped and John glanced around. Widow Kline meant well, but her scrutiny would make even a seasoned hunter nervous. She offered a faint, knowing smile. "You know, you could help her along. Show her how to hold it and all."

He withheld a groan and instead, rubbed the back of his neck. Yes, she could certainly crawl under even a grown man's skin and make them self-conscious.

"She does have a point." John ventured closer to Muireall. "If you do not mind, I can help you aim this time."

Her blue eyes widened, and her lips parted, but then she gave him another dip of her chin. "I am sure that would be acceptable. Considering the circumstances..." Muireall's gaze flitted to the back porch.

John chuckled. "Yes, after all, there is a chaperone present." With the mood lightened, he stepped up behind Muireall. Her slender body tucked nicely into his as he placed his hands over hers on the gun. With such dainty fingers, it was a miracle she handled the gun as well as she did. As soon as she learned to aim, she could be a formidable foe. He forced his mind from the soft scent of soap that lingered on her hair and how it tickled the side of his face as he lowered his head next to hers. His heart beat much too rapidly as he looked down the gun to the knot on the tree. "There," he breathed. Then, he eased his finger down over hers on the trigger.

The bullet landed just above the knot, but that was understandable considering his distraction. Muireall cleared her throat. He turned toward the sound, and his nose grazed over the softest of cheeks. John leapt backward, and the pistol clattered to the ground.

"Oh, I am so sorry. I can be so clumsy."

Despite her lame excuse, he was not a blind man. Far from it. Their closeness had flustered her as much as it had him. This woman was certainly dangerous, with or without a gun. At least when it came to his heart.

# CHAPTER 4

*March 25, 1784*

Never would she return. A chill swept through Muireall, despite the sunshine that bathed the countryside as they rode away from the fort. She turned in the saddle for one last look at the place she had called home these past few years, but it only resembled blurry brown boxes on the hillside behind her.

With a sigh, she faced the vast wilderness which stretched out before them. Her fingernails cut into the hard leather of the saddle as she gripped the pommel tighter. The old brown mare plodded down the hillside, head hung low. She had never ridden before, and she would prefer not to now, but her new husband had purchased the animal specifically for her. She could not snub his kind gesture, despite the apprehension he had easily picked up on as she stared up at the saddle. When he learned she had no experience with horses, he had assured her that he would lead the animal, as he did now.

In a way, it was a better arrangement than if she walked. John and the mare, named Sugar, would be mostly responsible for watching for obstacles Muireall might otherwise miss. But the ground was simply a green blob below, and her lack of depth perception made it seem as if she were fifty feet in the air rather than five. She frowned and focused on the round dark spot that was John's hat.

Muireall had seen little of him in the week between their odd engagement and the marriage that occurred earlier that morning, before they set out. With the weather blustery and dismal, John had honed his attentions on preparing for their journey while they awaited a turn for the better. He had checked in with her briefly each afternoon, though, and that simple attentiveness was heartening. But now, while it was John who had seemed unsure the day before last, it was she who could only muster trepidation and fear. Sometime through the night, memories of the journey to the fort had slipped into her consciousness. Memories of thunderstorms, rabid coyotes, life-threatening injuries, and a wide world she could not see.

How could anyone enjoy nature when they could not see well enough to relish its beauty? As it was now, she could feel the warmth of the bright sun upon her cheeks, but she could not tell how it gleamed off the blue-jay's bright feathers as she knew it had to. And though the grass boasted patches of brighter green, she could not distinguish blade from blade without kneeling close. Even the barren tree branches that loomed ahead only appeared as a tangle of gray. Meanwhile, Betty had raved over how purple and red buds dotted several of the trees within the fort. No, nature seemed more an obstacle than a blessing when in unfamiliar territory as they would be.

Perhaps focusing on her husband rather than herself would prove a distraction. Should she not try to get to know this man she was married to, after all? Raising her voice to be heard where he walked alongside Sugar's head, she asked the first question that came to mind. "Where do ye hail from, John?" His name still felt new and strange upon her lips. But it was only right to call her husband by his Christian name.

He glanced her direction. "Virginia."

"Really? Us too. Whereabouts in Virginia?" Could they have grown up near one another? She tried to imagine what he might have looked like as a youngster. Had he always worn an eyepatch, or had he sustained an injury? The scars on his face hinted at the latter.

John cleared his throat. "Along the Potomac, near the sea."

"Ah. We lived near the mountains. It was such lovely country, and we never seemed to have any dire needs. I never understood why Pa wanted to leave and come west." Muireall frowned. What she could remember about the home she grew up in was agreeable, but her eyesight had begun to diminish at such a young age, were her memories truly accurate? Or had she clung so tightly to the images of the wildflowers that grew at the edge of the woods that she had neglected to remember the parts that were not as pleasant? Of course, there could have been matters that a child would not understand. Or that her mother had sheltered her from.

From the moment Ma had learned of her poor eyesight, she had kept her nestled under her wing. Muireall's heart still ached to consider her death. It seemed that over and over in her life, she had been thrust into new and unsettling situations. When she became comfortable with her circumstances, life would be turned on its head. Perhaps that was life, though. After all, was it not Ecclesiastes that said, *To everything there is a season, and a time to every purpose under the heaven?*

Still, this new season had her on edge. Her gaze drifted to her husband again. He did not seem to notice that she had fallen silent. His own focus was cast ahead, to the wild woods that would constitute a good part of their journey. Did he think of who he was in search of in the way she spent much time thinking of her sister? And who was this mysterious person? A family member? A lover? Her chest constricted, but she pushed the thought from her mind. John did not seem the kind to take one woman, only to go in search of another one.

Still, his secrecy was a bit unnerving. Especially considering how their marriage came to be and the uncertain terms of their union. Why had she not clarified before they were wed? Muireall stifled a groan. She had been so bent on going to her sister and so shy around her mysterious groom that she had never defined the nature of their marriage. John had given her the choice, laid it at her feet, and she had neglected to acknowledge the gift. Now, it was a looming unknown that hung between them. Did John see their marriage as one in name only? A weight settled in her stomach at the thought. While she had been apprehensive about marrying someone of whom she knew so little, she had been grateful for the union and hopeful for their future.

As they moved down the hill and into the woods, dead leaves from the winter past crunched under Sugar's hooves. Twigs snapped under John's steps, and Muireall took heart that it was not she who had to navigate the hidden dips and grooves which could snag her step. Meanwhile, even though he was quiet, John marched confidently ahead. When they approached a stream, he stopped and pulled out the map, surveying both it and their surroundings. Then, after he tucked the map back into his chest pocket, he cast a quick glance her way before forging ahead. If only she could see well enough to read his expression. *Lord, why do I have to be afflicted so?*

Muireall suppressed a sigh. For now, there was nothing else to do but to be blindly led into the great unknown.

~

*T*here. John's gaze landed on a thick stand of pines at the base of the hill they traveled down. It should provide adequate shelter from the elements. He glanced to where Muireall sat atop Sugar, her spine stiff and her jaw clenched. His mouth pulled to the side. He should have known better than to ask a full day's travel of her right away. Such a feat would be uncomfortable for even an experienced rider. "We will make camp there, among the pines." He pointed to the trees as he led the mare in their direction.

Muireall gave a silent nod. Once they reached the stand, the mare was more than glad to come to a halt. She let out a long breath that ruffled her lips before he turned to help Muireall down. Muireall slid to the ground, then wavered, her fingers digging into his arm through his coat. Once her eyes focused, their deep blue gaze locked onto his face and her grip loosened. But still, her touch bore into his arm through his layers. The temperature of the day seemed to rise at her nearness. And for the briefest moment, she seemed to lean into him. Then she abruptly turned to the packs, lifting one from the horse. "Where shall the fire be?"

John hesitated, his mind still reeling from the

sudden shift. He turned and motioned to a place in the middle of the stand. "There." His voice came out raspier than normal. He cleared his throat before he busied himself with unloading the rest of their wares.

Muireall settled the pack of food near where he indicated and moved to collecting wood. She bent for a broken pine branch.

His brow lowered. The pine would smoke them out if they attempted to burn it. Perhaps his wife was not used to selecting her own wood, only feeding the fire with what was provided. John stepped to her side and laid a hand on her arm to stop her. "Pine does not burn well, because of the sap. The oak over here will be much better." He indicated the ground below an old oak tree, where several dead limbs had crashed to the ground and broken into pieces. They would provide a good start for the fire, and he could gather more wood once he had watered the mare.

"Oh." Muireall frowned and moved to where he pointed.

John finished unloading the mare and dug out a pot before he went in search of water. Just down from their camp was a small stream with crystal-clear water tumbling over smooth creek rocks. When he dipped his hand in to splash his face, the water was colder than expected for the time of year. "Must be fed by a spring," he told Sugar, who seemed glad to lower her mouth to the cold liquid. John settled on his heels and allowed the mare a thorough drink before he dipped a pot of water and headed back for Muireall.

"The creek must be spring-fed. It is as cold and clear as can be." It was surprising how naturally his smile came at the sight of her leaned over the fire, her long hair a curtain of black over her back.

"Thank you." Muireall smiled up at him as she accepted the pot.

He tied the horse and settled in beside her as she poured water into their two tin cups. It did not escape his notice that she filled his first. The water slowly rose ever closer to the rim of the cup. Then tipped over the side.

"Oh!" Muireall gasped when the dirt beside the cup darkened. John chuckled.

"All is well." He lifted the cup, and very carefully, took a sip. The cool liquid was a balm to his parched throat.

Still, Muireall blew out a frustrated breath before she pushed the smile back onto her face. "I believe I will prepare us a hearty stew."

John nodded his assent. He could have sufficed the week's journey on salted ham and jerked meat, but he had brought some perishable goods along for his wife. It was easy enough to tell, though, by the look on her face, that she made the stew for him, not for herself. Her mouth was drawn and her eyes weary as she stood to gather supplies.

As she moved between him and the fire, her petticoat billowed into the fire. "Muireall!" John leapt forward. Muireall turned and cried out at the sight of the small flame that ate at the edge of her garment. John latched onto the fabric and stood, stomping on the flame to put it out.

When he met Muireall's gaze, her eyes were wide and her breathing heavy. "Thank ye," she whispered.

John's heartbeat pounded in his ears as he stared down at her. "You must be careful," he urged gently.

Like a book being slammed shut, Muireall closed up. Her mouth clamped shut, and she gave a quick nod before she turned back to the task of gathering supplies for stew. John sighed. He had not intended to anger her.

What did he expect? For several years, he had lived under the illusion that he had turned his life around. But he knew the truth. He was no good and would never make a decent husband. Inside, he was still the same good-for-nothing that the kids had seen all those years ago. A growl came from his throat, deep and guttural. Muireall whipped to him.

"Sorry," he muttered. "I need to take a walk..." He searched for an excuse.

"To relieve myself."

"Aye." Muireall nodded and averted her gaze.

John sighed and left. Why had he roped him and Muireall into this sham of a marriage? To save her from the humiliation and shame of becoming like his mother? To protect her virtue? What good would it do her when she learned the truth? When she learned who and what she was married to? The questions were coming. It was a matter of time. People always asked. *How did you get that eyepatch? What happened to your eye?* An accident when he was a kid, was all he would ever say. When they pressed for details, he said he would rather not discuss it.

He scoffed. "An accident." It was no accident when his boyhood classmates had spewed words of hate and pummeled him with stones because of his illegitimate birth. As if he had any control in the matter. That was when he learned that no matter what he did, he could not rise above his circumstances. And eventually, it was why he moved west and adopted a new name. At Fort Harrod, he had become a new man. People accepted him.

But it was all an illusion, wasn't it?

A movement caught John's eye and jerked him from his self-pity. John peered at the tree line on the hill above him. The trees were too dense, but was that a man? John's heart kicked up a notch. He shook his head and peered again. No, just darkness. Surely, it was a trick of the mind. Still, a prickle up the back of his neck set him on a course back to camp, and to his wife.

# CHAPTER 5

*M*uireall stood and shifted her weight from one foot to the other. She had held this business off as long as she could. "I need to take a quick walk," she advised her husband as she stepped away from the fire.

"I will join you." John was to his feet before Muireall could protest, and her shoulders sagged.

As much as she appreciated his sudden attentiveness and did not wish to venture into the darkness alone, this matter could not have an audience. Even her husband. Muireall placed a hand on his arm. "Alone," she appended, her voice firm and her brow raised.

John hesitated and looked from her to woods behind her. "It is dark and dangerous." His hat cast a shadow over his face.

Muireall fidgeted. The man still did not understand

her insinuation, and she could not wait much longer. "John, I need to relieve meself."

"Oh."

"Aye," Muireall confirmed, then, without further conversation, turned and ventured into the trees. She only wandered as far as necessary to hide her personal matters from her husband. She hurried past several trees before ducking behind a large oak.

As soon her business was complete, she stood and straightened her petticoats. Suddenly, it was as though the darkness enveloped her and swallowed her whole. It was hard enough to see during the day, but at night, dark blurred into dark and just created an endless black. Muireall closed her eyes and took a deep breath in an attempt to slow her rapidly beating heart. Then she turned and stepped from behind the tree. The light of the campfire broke though the darkness, providing a small haze of orange that she could focus on. Moving forward, she tripped on a stick. She quickly righted herself and kept moving toward the light. As she stumbled past the last pine, arms latched onto her.

Muireall gasped and jumped, but as she looked up, she relaxed into the strong grip. 'Twas only John.

"Is all well?" He glanced from her to the woods behind her.

Muireall nodded, but her mind was far from the woods. Instead, she was lost in the nearness of her husband. There was something about his body so close to hers that made it difficult to breathe and sent warm tingles skittering across her skin. Firelight flickered across his features, his square jaw and the dark hair that peeked from below his hat. She brought her hand up to his cheek and rubbed her thumb over the scars that riddled his face. What had happened to this man? Still, despite his somewhat roguish appearance, Muireall felt safe in his arms. As if it was exactly where she belonged and his strength could protect her from the world. Had God brought her a helpmate who could see her through life and be her proverbial eyes?

John engulfed her hand in his, removing it from where it still lingered against his face but not breaking contact with her. Heat rippled through her before John cleared his throat and stepped away. He kept a hand at her elbow, but a chasm seemed to have opened between them.

"We should get some rest." John motioned to where he had laid out a stack of furs and quilts to create a makeshift bed on the ground near the fire.

Muireall nodded. Would he expect her to act as a wife tonight? Surely not, considering she had not indicated that she wished for that kind of marriage. Still, she swallowed at the thought, then tucked herself under the top quilt and waited for her husband to join her. When he did, John slid an arm beneath her head and tugged her close to his body. But he made no move to kiss her or take the action further, so she nestled in for the night and savored the warmth that radiated between them. Perhaps the closeness of her husband would banish her nightmares. For the first time in weeks, Muireall settled in for sleep with a smile on her face.

~

*MARCH 26, 1784*

John jerked awake and looked around. Though the first light of dawn peeked over the horizon, the morning was quiet and still. The dark form of the old mare slumbered nearby, and Muireall's soft breaths came in a slow, even rhythm. He frowned. All seemed at peace, but a dissonance within kept him from relaxing. Unable to shake the sensation, he carefully removed his numb right arm from beneath his wife and stood. If he could not sleep, there was nothing else to do but to break camp.

He went over and unhobbled the mare. "Come on, girl." He rasped the words as he attempted to lift her heavy head to replace her bridle. The animal groaned as if in protest and lifted her head only long enough to scrub it against his shoulder. John sighed and leaned down to slip the bridle over her nose. The poor horse was well beyond her working years, but she was all he had been able to afford after paying Rollinson for the map. Finally, he coaxed her toward the creek, rifle in hand.

Once she was watered, John turned her toward camp and headed back through the woods.

"John?" Muireall's voice broke through the quiet morning and quickened the beating of his heart.

He urged the mare faster. "Muireall?" He stepped through the trees to find his wife standing beside the pallet of furs and blankets. She turned at the sound of his voice, and her demeanor relaxed.

"There ye are." She smiled and took a step toward him, then stopped.

"I went to water the mare," John explained as he led Sugar over to where the saddle and supplies laid in a heap. "I would prefer to head out as soon as you are ready." When he turned to Muireall, she nodded.

Less than a half hour later, they were on the move. John had yet to find any indication that someone was trailing them, yet he glanced over his shoulder every so often. Clouds gathered overhead, casting a dreariness over the day and tightening the knot in his middle. A cool wind snaked about his neck as he stopped at a creek to check the map. He looked all around, but only newly budded trees intermixed with a smattering of pines surrounded them. He shook his head and led the mare through the shallow water and on about their way. Still, the sensation that someone was watching him followed.

Ignoring it, John trudged on. If the weather would hold, they could make it to Rolling Fork River and cross today. If anyone was following them, surely, the river crossing would deter them. Only someone truly dedicated would risk it without due reason. Right?

~

*M*uireall gasped as Sugar stumbled beneath her, her front end suddenly dipping down and throwing Muireall off balance.

"Ho, girl," John called to the mare through the rain, but she had already righted herself.

'Twas only Muireall's heart that needed steadied now.

Steady rain fell all around them, overwhelming her senses. The rhythm of it drumming against the earth filled her ears while the barrage of droplets further blurred her already poor vision. Her fingers curled in stiff fists around the reins, and she shivered against the chill that seeped through her dampened clothes. Should they not have sought shelter at the first sign of rain rather than pressing on? And yet, the bottom portions of her petticoats were soaked along with her hair, and water seeped beneath the collar of her coat, threatening to do the same to her bodice.

At the bottom of the hill, John stopped. He seemed to survey their surroundings as he ran a hand over his jaw. But for Muireall, all was enveloped in a gray haze. When John glanced her way, she forced a smile, though it could not have been a convincing one. Muireall's heart dropped when John turned and plowed forward again.

This time, he marched up the hillside at an angle, his gaze affixed straight ahead. Muireall closed her eyes. Cold liquid splattered against her face, and her body swayed with the horses' movements, her saddle-sore behind protesting with every step. Muireall stifled a groan.

"Here we are."

Her eyes popped open at her husband's voice. Muireall's brow furrowed while she attempted to make out the outline of rocks and hillside where they had come to a stop.

"We will camp here under this overhang," John explained at her hesitation. "There will not be enough room for Sugar, but perhaps we can dry ourselves with a small fire."

Muireall nodded, then held onto the pommel as she carefully lowered herself from the saddle. John came up beside her and guided her under the large rock that would provide their shelter. The giant boulder protruded from the earth, providing perfect protection underneath, even if one had to crouch in order to gain entrance. Muireall settled on the dry dirt floor, grateful for a reprieve from the wind and rain.

After a moment, John appeared at her side again. He wrapped a fur around her shoulders. "I will unload Sugar, then see if I can find some wood dry enough to burn. Remain here and stay as warm as you can."

Muireall's mouth dropped open as he moved away, but then she clamped it shut, holding her words inside. Though the thought of being left alone made it difficult to breathe, she could not voice her fears. Could not explain. Nay, she would appear the dutiful, obedient wife while secretly praying that John was not away long. Muireall closed her eyes and forced air into her lungs, then released it as she drew the fur tighter around her. She needed to pray. Prayer would settle her soul. A lesson she had learned on the journey to the fort, but seemed to have forgotten.

*Lord, please calm me anxious mind. Please bring Yer peace upon me, an' allow me to trust in Yer protection. Cover us with Yer wings of protection, an' keep us from harm.* She took another deep breath. *An' Lord, please help me an' John to find our way in our marriage. Please help our union grow into a loving marriage, an' show me how to be a good wife. One who is not afraid of the world an' all she cannae see. Please be me eyes Lord.*

Muireall opened her eyes, and peace settled over her despite the fact that her clothing remained damp and cold and rain still poured all around. The time until John returned with an armload of wood passed quickly. He huffed out a breath as he slipped into the shelter. "I am not sure any of it is dry enough to burn. I should have been collecting wood at the first sign of rain."

"All will be well," she assured him as she moved alongside him. Suddenly, the shelter seemed diminished in size. "At least we have one another to keep us warm." Muireall bit her lip as John stilled. But then he faced her with a soft smile.

"That we do," he agreed before he turned back to the logs.

She shifted to help block the wind as he attempted to bring a flame to life, but no matter how they tried, the damp wood would not do more than smolder and smoke. John sat back on his heels with a growl. Muireall frowned.

"Perhaps we can eat a bite an' then try again?"

"I would be amenable to that." John practically sighed the words, fatigue heavy in his voice.

Muireall placed her hand on his and gave it a squeeze. Unlike hers, his fingers were warm, and the heat penetrated her skin. She quickly released his hand and turned to the packs. Their meals for the day had been a monotonous selection of the same jerked meat, but at least their bellies were full. Perhaps, come morning, there would be fire enough for a substantial meal.

Muireall sat beside her husband and ate in silence. Within minutes, they were both finished, and an awkwardness seemed to have settled between them. If only she had clarified her intentions for their marriage, perhaps they would have some inkling of how to proceed despite the newness of their union. Instead, loneliness wrapped around her like a heavy cloak even with her husband so near.

Muireall fetched her sewing from the packs and set to work. She knew nothing else to fill the void, and while he was not privy to the knowledge, she labored on a shirt for her new husband. Not only was the rhythmical sewing comforting, but mayhap if she acted as a caring, dutiful wife, her husband would understand her desire for a full marriage and fill the role of a husband. She chanced a glance his way as he laid back on the dirt floor, his head reaching the rock at the head of the shelter despite his legs being bent in a V. She smiled as he tipped his hat forward and tucked his arms under his head. He was not an unattractive man. His frame was strong and solid, and he was tall without being overly so. In fact, he would be quite appealing in the chestnut-brown fabric she worked. And with little else to do until sleep lured her, she might be able to finish the project within the day. Perhaps presenting him with the gift would start them off on the right foot the next morning?

# CHAPTER 6

*J*ohn jerked awake and blinked into the darkness. A cold chill shook his body, and he groaned. He had only meant to close his eyes for a moment, not to sleep well into the night. Now cool air cloaked his face instead of his hat, and Muireall curled against his chest. But as he wrapped his arm tighter around her thin frame, he realized she had pulled the furs and blankets over them before settling in for the night.

At least his wife had the foresight to provide such protection. But with the drop in temperatures the rain had brought, it would behoove him to attempt a small fire again. The last thing he wanted was for Muireall to catch a chill, or worse, on his account.

Carefully extricating himself from beneath her, he slid over to where their pile of wood still waited. In the dark, it still took several tries to coax a flame to life, but soon a small orange whisp broke through the night.

John rubbed his hands together, then worked to grow the flame into a substantial enough fire.

"John?" Muireall's voice, raspy from sleep, garnered his attention. When he turned, she blinked at him from under a furrowed brow.

"The air has taken on a chill. I thought it best for us to have a fire now that the wood has dried enough."

Muireall nodded and sidled up next to him. Then she laid her head on his shoulder and closed her eyes once more. John's chest squeezed as he took in her pale features in the flickering firelight. How had he come to be married to this beautiful woman with skin the color of pale porcelain? He swallowed. And how could he ever be good enough for her?

She must have sensed him watching her, for Muireall tipped her face up to him. Her smile lifted her lips in an attractive curve, and John's mouth went dry. But as the thought of kissing those sweet lips slipped into his mind, she sat up suddenly.

"Oh, I have a surprise for ye!"

John blinked and followed her actions as she moved over to their stack of supplies and withdrew brown fabric. She returned to his side and laid what appeared to be a garment in his lap. He lifted it and carefully held it up in the light of the fire. Muireall had made a shirt... for him. "You made this?"

She bit her lip and nodded, her face expectant, as

though she was unsure of his reaction. Meanwhile, he was left stunned. He could not remember the last time anyone had spent time and effort on something for him, simply out of the goodness of their heart. "I apologize if 'twas presumptuous of me." Muireall's gaze fell to her lap. "I had the fabric an' needed a task to keep me hands from bein' idle."

"Muireall." His voice was husky as he dropped the garment in his lap and took her small hand into his. He rubbed his thumb over the back of her knuckles, coaxing her gaze to his. "I appreciate it more than you could ever know."

She gave him a demure smile, and the warmth that spread through him matched the flush that colored her face. His heart was in dangerous territory. He ran the back of his fingers along the edge of her jaw and over the silken skin of her neck. Despite the risks, he longed to explore this new territory. John swallowed. Muireall had never said whether there marriage would be more than in name alone. But the blue eyes that watched him were wide and curious and seemed to beckon him like the crystal-clear waters of a spring on a long, scorching summer day.

Slowly, John lowered his lips to Muireall's and she lifted her face to meet his. Her kiss was softer and sweeter than anything he had ever experienced in life, so deliciously perfect that it stirred an ache deep inside. His hand drifted into her hair, and his other arm went around her waist as she melded further into him. How exquisite could life be if he entrusted his heart into this woman's care?

John forced himself to pull back and take a breath. No, it was not as simple as that. He could not fall for her. Not when she was in the dark regarding his past. And no woman could love him once she knew the truth. He pressed one last kiss to her forehead before gently setting her aside. "You should get some rest."

Without meeting her gaze, he nodded toward the pile of furs and blankets where they had slept. Muireall, ever proving herself the dutiful wife, did as he instructed. But not before he caught a glimpse of the hurt and uncertainty that flashed across her face. She likely thought she had done something wrong to bring about his change in demeanor. John closed his eyes and ignored the unrest in his middle. Would he still ruin this lovely woman?

*March 27, 1784*

*A* shiver coursed through Muireall's body as the waters of the Rolling Fork River roared along before them. Memories of her last crossing flashed in her mind. Of how pale and weak Margaret's husband had been before the crossing, after his brush with death. *Lord, Ye delivered us across then. Please do so again.*

When John's boots crunched on the rocks beside

her, she turned to look up at him. Stones skittered into the water as Sugar plodded up on his other side, head held low to the ground. Could the poor animal even make it across with such a strong current? Iain's strong palomino had been instrumental in their crossing when they traveled to the fort. But Sugar was aged, with protruding hips and gray sprinkled across her back.

Muireall swallowed. Could she make it across alone?

John seemed to sense her hesitation. His strong hand slipped into hers, and she leaned into him as tender memories of the night before drifted to the forefront of her mind. Though it had ended abruptly, the intimacy of the moment had spoken to a connection being weaved between husband and wife. One she desired to further. If only she had not made whatever mistake had broken the reverie.

John glanced behind them and squeezed her hand. "We should cross."

"Are ye sure 'tis safe?" Why did it always seem to storm prior to this river crossing?

"Sugar and I will go first. Then I will ensure that you make it across safely." With him at her side and his hand laced with hers, his determination reached to her core, reassuring her.

John released her hand and untied his rope from the saddle. He turned and pulled a loop down over her head, securing it at her waist. "I will carry the other end across with me," he explained as he tied it to the saddle. "Then I will use the rope to guide you over."

Muireall looked up into her husband's face. When had such a roguish appearance come to be so comforting? And how had it happened so quickly? But the lone brown eye that peered down at her was filled with compassion and assurance. Defying the distance he had put between them the night before, she tipped up onto her toes and pressed a quick, soft kiss to his lips. Then she willingly stepped from his grip.

John turned and, without a moment's hesitation, strode into the water. *Lord, please see them safely across.* Slowly, John and Sugar moved lower and lower in the water, until their heads were simply dark splotches in a sea of blue and white. Still it seemed the river carried them downriver as quickly as they could cross. Muireall's fingers pressed into the rope at her middle.

The rope jerked her forward, and she gasped. John had not reached the shore already, had he? But as she scanned the far bank of the river, brown blurred into brown and she could not be sure. Yet the rope continued to tug her forward, her shoes splashing into the shallow water even as she resisted. There! A movement downriver caught her attention, and the rope slackened.

"I will draw you across in a moment, Muireall. Stay right there." John's voice from across the river aligned with where it appeared he and Sugar were making their way back upriver. She watched their movement, the sound of the rushing water filling her ears. Once they were directly across from her, he called, "We are ready."

*Lord, please go with me.*

One step at a time, Muireall eased forward, the cold water seeping through her layers of petticoats and her thick wool stockings. She sucked in her middle as it reached her waist, and a small gasp escaped when it claimed her chest. With her chin barely above the water even with her stretched on her tiptoes, there was no doubt the next step would take her from solid ground. The rush of the water pushed at her body, making it impossible to stay in place. Yet still, she fought it, her old fears overwhelming her, and a whimper escaped. Was the rope still tight at her waist, or had it slipped free, leaving her helpless?

"Muireall, you have to swim."

Muireall swallowed and closed her eyes as she stepped forward, deeper into the cold liquid. She gulped a lungful of air and lashed out at the river. She kicked and flailed, barely able to keep her head above the water as it pulled her along.

"Muireall, I have you." John's voice cut through her panic. "Just keep your eyes on me."

Muireall shoved herself above the water and affixed her gaze to the blur on the shore that she knew to be John. She cut her arms through the water. She had done this once before, and she could do it again. *Lord, deliver me across safely.*

As Muireall swam with all her strength, the rope at

her waist propelled her gently forward against the current which tried to pull her downstream. But even as she floated on past her husband and his horse, she kept her eyes on him. Slowly, she drew closer, and his form grew larger and clearer. She pushed onward, toward the hat-clad man who was her husband and became more of a comfort to her each day.

Finally, her feet found purchase once more. She used her legs to push up and out of the water, onto the shore. As Muireall sloshed from the water's edge, she immediately went to her husband without thought. Relief flooding her, she wrapped him in a sopping-wet hug. She trembled as she clung to his sturdy frame, to the anchor that had guided her across.

*Thank ye, Lord, for seein' me safely over, an' thank Ye for this man.*

~

John forgot the chill of the air as he wrapped his arms around his wife. Her raven-haired head laid against his chest as tremors shook her slender body. A desperate need to protect her and care for her coursed through him, causing him to hold her tighter as he scanned the far shore for danger. He had not seen a single hint that anyone followed them since that first day, but he still wanted to be careful. John set Muireall away from him and tipped up the corner of his mouth in a grin. "Let us remove that rope from you."

In response, Muireall graced him with the prettiest smile. One that made his insides twist. He ignored the sensation as he fumbled with the rope. Finally, he loosened the loop, and slid it over Muireall's head. "We should travel a ways and then set up camp somewhere safe where we can start a warm fire."

Muireall nodded, though she still shivered.

He nodded toward where Sugar picked at a patch of grass. "Would you like to ride?"

Muireall glanced at the saddle, then out at the forest in front of them as though she were weighing her options. Her mouth crimped before she looked down at her sodden clothes. She bent forward and squeezed water from the layers and layers of fabric. Then she stood tall, her eyes flashing with a confidence that he had not seen in her before. It caused the corner of his mouth to tip up again. "I will walk."

John took up the reins in one hand and Muireall's hand in the other. He led them forward as the warm sunshine knocked the chill off of the wind that whipped at them. He had to admit that after so many years of keeping to himself, it was nice to have a companion to share this journey with. If only he could share everything with her. A vice tightened around his chest.

# CHAPTER 7

*J*ohn tied the last corner of the skin in place, effectively erecting a shelter against the relentless wind.

Muireall let out a sigh and rubbed her upper arms. "That should make it a bit easier to make a fire." She offered him a tired smile with her reassuring words.

He moved closer and gave her arm a gentle squeeze. Her clothes were still damp from the river crossing, as his were. "Have a seat," he urged her. "I will start the fire."

While she had been brave, it was evident the days' events had been taxing on Muireall. John had to admit that even he was drained, though. The Rolling Fork River, coupled with the recent rains and persistent wind, had not been easy to overcome.

He knelt and stacked the logs, weaving in the kindling. He had not let Muireall on as to how difficult the crossing had been. It would have only heightened her fears and wounded her trust in him to know that for a moment, he was not sure he and Sugar were going to successfully make it to the far side. The river had pulled him and the horse downriver with such force, it had been overwhelming. But knowing Muireall waited for him to see her across had kept him pushing on.

As the fire sprang to life, he stood and dusted his hands on his breeches. John turned and busied himself with rearranging their packs. Anything to distance himself, and his heart, from Muireall. Somehow, he had to shift his focus back to the original task at hand—finding his father. Once John knew who he was, perhaps then he could settle down with his wife and make a life. He had become so engrossed with her safety, he had lost sight of his goal. But maybe a shift in focus could help keep him from falling?

The object of his thoughts appeared at his side, capturing his attention once again. "I thought a nice stew might do us well tonight," she said as she dug into their food packs.

"Uh, yes. Yes, that would be good." He nodded as she retreated with a grin. John hung his head.

Muireall gave of herself each day, putting visible effort into their marriage, while he fought to keep his distance. It was not right, but what could he do? He could not give this version of himself to his wife. And he could not tell her the truth.

*MARCH 28, 1784*

The brilliant red splashed across the sky marked the drawing to an end of a most pleasant day. Bright rays had graced their journey from dawn until the sun dropped behind the trees. Warmth seeped through their clothing and bathed the world in light. It was the kind of day which Muireall favored, on which she could see the best. On such days as this, the lights seemed lighter and the darks darker, more distinct. And the sunshine infused joy into her soul. Even the mare seemed to have more energy, her brown head bobbing as she eagerly followed John uphill and down. Muireall had forgotten how the Kentucky landscape was ever-changing, rising and lowering at every turn. At the moment, they approached a tree line after cutting through a small meadow.

A flash of brown darted across in front of them. The old mare jerked her head into the air and halted abruptly. Muireall's heart lurched into her throat. "John?" Apprehension filled her voice.

John turned toward her. Was he smiling? "'Twas only a bobcat. More afraid of us than us of him."

"Oh." Muireall nodded while mentally giving herself a swift kick. Though there were dangerous animals in the Kentucky wilderness that required a measure of caution, she should have hidden her fear better. "I dinnae get a good glimpse of him."

"He was quick," John agreed before he led Sugar on.

Muireall released her breath, her shoulders sagging. She should not have to lie and make excuses to her husband, should she? It did not seem right, but Ma had kept the secret of her eyesight from her father. Perhaps it was the way of the world, men thinking less of women with a weakness. After all, her mither had been quite convinced that no one would want her should they know the truth. Would Pa not have wanted her as his child if he had been privy to the situation? Would John cast her aside if he learned the truth? Her mouth twisted at the thought, and a cold chill swept over her.

She tried to shake the gloom as John led them over the next rise and down another, but no matter how the countryside around them greened with the coming spring, discomfort and fear still swirled inside.

"That rock wall should make for a decent place to camp for the night." John guided them to a place where it seemed the Lord had taken a giant knife and cut away a piece of the earth as He had formed it. Layers of pale stone formed a wall that stretched higher than her head. A mound of tree-covered earth rested at its top, and the terrain sloped down on each side.

When she dismounted, John was there with his hand at the small of her back. Though she no longer needed his assistance after the past few days of mounting and dismounting, she did relish the warmth of his touch and the nearness of him. The world did not seem so frightening with him around. Muireall smiled up at him. "I believe I am learnin'."

"That you are," he concurred with a lift of his own lips. His smile eased the hard edges of his face and brought a light to his left eye.

Muireall raised her hand and gently brushed her thumb along his cheek below his eyepatch. He stilled. "Does it hurt?" She breathed the words.

"No. I..." He cleared his throat. "I still have the eye. Only, it was injured and I cannot see out of it. This...this is easier for people to understand."

Muireall nodded, but her heart clenched. If only it were easier for people to understand her deficit, then maybe they would accept her as they did John. But he still had one working eye. Neither of hers worked proficiently. Perhaps that was the difference. "What...what happened?"

John's gaze slid away from hers, and his jaw worked. "I would rather not say." His voice was tight, pained. Most likely, the memories were too haunting to revisit.

She could not blame him for not wanting to relive such an experience. She took his face into her hands, drawing his focus back to her. "Whatever it is, it does not matter. Ye are a handsome an' wonderful man, exactly as ye are." Conviction filled her words. While she may have only known him eight short days, she believed with all her heart that he was a good man. One she was glad to call her husband.

John's adam's apple bobbed as he swallowed. Then the corners of his mouth turned down.

Muireall's brow furrowed. Had she said something wrong or crossed a line?

"Thank you, Muireall," he finally said as he stepped away from her. "I...need to go water the horse."

Though she dipped her chin in assent, her face remained taut with confusion.

John walked down the slope in search of a creek with the mare still laden with their supplies. They always removed the saddle and packs before taking her to find water.

Muireall turned and took a deep breath as she flopped her arms at her sides. She supposed all that was left for her to do was to collect firewood. She gathered the small twigs and branches closest to her, as well as some dead leaves for kindling. Then, leaving them at camp, she broadened her search for substantial logs that would sustain the fire. She approached the base of a tall oak and knelt where, beyond a patch of green moss, dead leaves were hidden under blades of grass and tiny pinkish flowers. She reached under the flowers for a thick piece of branch that was nestled there.

Suddenly, it was as though the back of her hand was on fire. Muireall let out a scream, dropping what little wood she had gathered as she jerked her hand back. She cradled it to her chest as pain seared across it. The skin was not broken, but a long red line marred the flesh as though tiny flames were trapped inside and trying to burn their way out.

John crashed through the underbrush and knelt by her side, his breathing heavy. His touch was gentle as he took her hand into his to examine it. Then he surveyed the plants which she had reached into. "There." John used a stick to push one of the flower stems back. But Muireall could not make out whatever insect he revealed, nor did she much care. It did not matter what the tiny foe appeared like, for it did not make it any less painful. "The spines on that caterpillar will eat you alive. Are there any still stuck in your hand?"

"I dinnae think so."

John turned his attention back to her hand. "I do not see any. Here, come to the creek. The cool water might help."

He slipped an arm around her as she rose and guided her down to the creek, her arm still cradled in his hand. When he dipped her hand into the cold liquid, she barely contained a whimper, tears springing into her eyes. But after the initial shock, a bit of the intensity did slip away.

"Is that better?" John looked from her hand to her face. Muireall nodded. "Good. I have some salve that might be of use. Come."

He held her uninjured hand in his as he guided her back to camp. He led Sugar along on his other side, the patient mare having waited in place for his return. Once she was settled on the ground, he dug a tin from one of the saddle packs. "It is old, so I am not sure how well it will work now. But it used to."

Something in his voice whispered of days past. Could this have been the very salve that helped heal the injuries to his face? She longed to have him open up to her and share the details of his background with her, but of course, she did not want to force him to recall the memories if they were too painful. So, instead, she whispered a soft, "Thank you," as he rubbed the soothing salve over the back of her hand.

"You rest here. I will gather some wood and start the fire." He paused and gave her a coy smile. "I might even prepare supper for you."

Muireall laughed. "Perhaps I should injure meself more often."

She sighed, her pain nearly forgotten as she watched his broad shoulders retreat down the hill. This kind of care and camaraderie was certainly easy to become accustomed to. Marriage with John seemed to suit her quite well. Though she had always known she was complete and whole with the Holy Spirit in her heart, that she needed no more than God, it was still as though a missing piece had been restored. A piece that she did not realize had been missing to begin with. It was much the same as when a dress was complete and whole, but then one added embroidery and adornment. Though the dress was perfect before, it could truly shine with the new additions.

Was that how God intended marriage? Aye, it was

right there in Ecclesiastes. *Two are better than one...and a threefold cord is not quickly broken.* There was a strength in a marriage built upon the Lord. Though she had prayed before allowing herself to be united with John, it was still astounding to consider that God had planned their sudden, strange marriage of convenience all along.

Muireall grinned. If God designed their meeting and union, He must have a plan for their future as well.

# CHAPTER 8

*MARCH 29, 1784*

Sunlight filtered through the trees and pulled John from the lull of sleep. He rolled up onto his elbow, facing Muireall where she slumbered next to him. Her raven hair spread across the deerskin beneath her, and her mouth was slightly parted. Over the last few days, her pale cheeks had taken on a rosy hue. He frowned. Before they set out, he should have made sure she had a cover, a hat or bonnet, to protect her skin from the elements. Most of the women in the fort worked outside nearly every day, helping with the planting, harvesting, and foraging, so he assumed she would be prepared. But his wife had spent the majority of her time indoors, sewing. Still, between the two of them, one would think they would have considered such a matter.

Muireall's forehead wrinkled before she blinked up at him. "Good mornin'?" Her voice rasped with the first use of the day.

"Good morning." John sat up to put some distance between them, but she followed suit.

"Is all well?"

John glanced toward her, then lifted the hat from his head and placed it atop hers. "Now it is."

Muireall's eyes widened, and her delicate hand went to her cheek. Then she dropped her gaze. "I...I should have thought to fashion a bonnet before our journey.

John caught his knuckle under her chin and tipped her face up to his. "You are beautiful, Muireall. I only want to spare you the pain I have seen others endure."

His wife blushed, the pink of her face deepening. "Will ye not need it?"

"I will survive." He flashed a grin in her direction before pushing to his feet.

Muireall rose as well and moved over to their packs, her head bent as she withdrew some salt-cured ham for them to start their day with. "I will set to work on a bonnet this verra afternoon when we make camp." The contriteness of her voice drew his attention.

John gave Muireall a long look. Though she wore her hair down and free, her bodice was intricately embroidered. In some ways, her appearance spoke of a genteel life, while in others, she seemed influenced by the wilderness of Kentucky. "How long did you live at the fort?"

"It would have been four years in June."

John nodded as he took the meat she offered, still not meeting his gaze. "And before that, you lived near Pitman Station? Where your sister is?"

"Aye. We had lived here in Kentucky for three years. Just long enough to lose both of our parents. Now I have lived here for a third of me life." Her mouth crimped. "But, with me sewin' an' all, I spent much of me time indoors, even then." She hurriedly added the last bit before she shoved a piece of ham into her mouth.

"Do you not like it here?"

Muireall shrugged. "It is home now, I suppose," was her reply, but she looked out into the woods and frowned.

John found himself moving closer. He touched her arm, drawing her attention to him. Though he was not sure he wanted to hear the answer, he asked, "If you could live anywhere, where would it be?"

Muireall whipped her gaze to him, and she blinked. "I dinnae know. I...miss me sister. I know that much."

A knife twisted in John's chest, and he scooted even closer to Muireall. He longed to ease the turmoil he had stirred in her expression. He put a hand to her soft cheek. "We will find her."

She offered him a smile in exchange for his declaration. It was small, as though she were still unsure of herself, but it held a trust and affection that he had never seen directed his way. It stole his breath. And in that moment, more than anything in the world, he wanted to be worthy of the love and acceptance that shone in those deep blue eyes. To be able to become lost in it and spend the rest of his life recreating it.

John sprang to his feet. "I need to water the mare." And put distance between him and his wife.

Loudly, he and the mare trudged down to the creek. When she lowered her head to the water, John did the same. Kneeling, he splashed cold water upon his face before running a hand through his hair.

What had become of him, and when had he lost sight of his goal, of finding his father? Could he lay down his own desires for those of his wife? He stood and paced a few feet away. The whole reason for his journey had been to locate his father, to finally gain the missing piece of the puzzle of who he was. And yet, that prospect now lacked luster in comparison to ensuring Muireall's happiness. An image of her beaming up at him after they discovered her sister safe and sound slipped into his mind and warmed the deep, dark place that he had kept hidden from the world.

John laid his arms across the horse's back and leaned his head down between them. Had the God that saved him years ago brought him a wife and given him a purpose in life? It could not be, could it? A broken, illegitimate child such as he?

*Can you still use me, Lord?*

He knew the answer before the prayer had even formed in his mind, but it did not seem possible. It was evident that Muireall needed him. He had not realized how ill-equipped she was for this wilderness they traversed. And he was glad to serve as the protector and to be the support she needed, but could she be all *he* needed? Was Muireall's husband who he was supposed to be?

He had trusted in God to guide him to his father, but he had never considered trusting God in any other capacity. Perhaps it was time.

~

John eased out his breath and rested his finger against the trigger. The rabbit lifted its head, but a sudden movement to its right caught his attention. John froze, his gaze darting to the motion. A man crept between one tree and another. A lanky man with a shock of blond hair hidden beneath a dark-colored hat bent to place a snare, then eased back into the shadows.

Rollinson.

John's mouth went dry. His heart thundered in his ears. His suspicions had been right all along. He had grown comfortable as he drew closer to Muireall and there had been no sign of followers since the river crossing. But now there was no doubt. For some reason, Rollinson and Hodges had trailed them for five days. With that kind of dedication, nothing good could come of it.

John had to get back to Muireall. Was she what they were after? He had seen the hungry gleam in Hodges's eyes that day at the fort. This was an awfully long, arduous trek just to take what one could from a woman, but what else could it be? He had little money to his name, for he had given most of it to them. Did they believe there was more where it came from, though? Greed could certainly propel a man. He had seen it before. But what would happen if they caught up to him and there was no money to be had?

John shuddered as he slipped between trees as quietly as possible. The consequences could be brutal. And Muireall could be injured, or worse—because of him.

No, he had to protect her at all cost. He would not sleep tonight. He would guard her, rifle at the ready. Then they would leave out at first light. If they pushed hard throughout the day, maybe they could gain some distance from their followers. And once they made camp, he would give Muireall another lesson with the pistol. She needed to be adept with a gun as well, in case Rollinson and Hodges were to catch her alone somehow...or should something happen to him.

Only once Muireall's beautiful voice singing a hymn met his ears did the tiniest amount of tension ease from John's shoulders. He walked right up to her and wrapped his arm around her waist, drawing her close. He needed her near.

Muireall let out a small squeak before she relaxed

into his embrace, her head nestling against his shoulder. He swallowed and held her tighter.

"John, is all well?"

When her voice came out strained, he realized he was squeezing her tighter than he meant to. He eased his grip and gently kissed her forehead. "Of course, it is."

Muireall pulled back and glanced down. "Did ye not find any game?"

"No. 'Tis a quiet night. There was one rabbit, but he darted away before I could pull the trigger."

"Mmm." Muireall curled back into his chest. "Ye can try again of a morrow if ye wish, but we have enough supplies to last to Pitman Station."

"True." But his mind was far from how they would fill their bellies over the next few days as he scanned the woods around them, his ear alert to even the tiniest sound out of place. *Lord, please help me keep her safe.*

# CHAPTER 9

*MARCH 30, 1784*

Thunder boomed overhead, and lightning flashed across the sky while rivulets of water ran down from the brim of John's hat. For the second night in a row, he pulled the rope taut that anchored the animal hide in place to form their shelter. This had to be the reason why so many travel parties coming west chose to travel in the winter. Despite the occasional snow or winter storm, the weather was much milder and more predictable in winter in Kentucky. Spring, instead, was proving to be the worst possible time for their journey. All around, the storm raged like a lion and he feared, if their shelter were to fail, it would ravage them.

John tested his knot one last time, then frowned as he dipped under the cover of the skin. Though he had done his best not to place them in the path of the streams that formed along the hillside, the ground where they were to bunk down for the night was sodden. There was no escape from the rainwater that rolled downhill, but had he truly chosen the best position? He glanced around, but no one could see through the squall.

Muireall latched onto his arm and urged him to sit beside her on the fur where she and the supplies took refuge from the muck. "Come. Get out of that rain, or ye'll catch yer death."

Though she fussed over him, it was she that shivered, her skin paler than usual. Despite having borrowed his hat, her dark hair was plastered against her chest and shoulders. John withdrew a blanket and fur and wrapped both around her. He tucked her close, then rubbed his thumb over her cold cheek. He had to get her warmed. At least he had managed to collect some wood throughout the day. Now he prayed it would burn in such damp conditions.

After making use of his flint and steel, John held one hand up to protect the fragile flame while he shifted the kindling. Slowly, he coaxed it to life. But even as he resumed his position at Muireall's side, the fire sputtered and spit as the wind tossed rain into the shelter. His wife curled into him as her shivering slowed to a stop. His own chill seemed to have subsided, and a sigh escaped. He pushed his hat back on his head and pressed his cheek against Muireall's hair.

Even with the constant booms overhead and the roar of the torrential rainfall, it felt right to have his wife tucked under his arm. Righter than nearly anything he had experienced in life. But if he wanted to cultivate this union, he would have to be honest with Muireall. About everything.

John closed his eyes and leaned upon the only one who could see them through what had to happen. *Lord, please open Muireall's heart to me. When I am honest with her, please allow her to be forgiving. At least in time. Please do not let my mistakes destroy what has been built between us. Please do not let me extinguish this blessing which you have brought to life.*

Muireall turned in his arms and tipped her face up to his, drawing his attention. "Our travel seems to be thwarted at every turn."

His heart clenched. If she only knew. Was this the moment? Before he could speak, she placed her delicate hand upon the side of his face.

"All will be well," she whispered, and he felt it to his core. "As long as I am with ye, all will be well."

John closed his eyes and leaned his forehead against Muireall's. How did this woman know exactly what his heart craved to hear? Her soft voice whispered to the innermost broken places within him, covering them with her love and acceptance. "Oh, Muireall," he breathed, considering how he would have to break her heart. He hugged her closer, resting his chin atop her head. He should not delay the inevitable, but he could not bring himself to break the moment. To sever the precious bond that had been forged between them. *Lord, help me.*

~

*MARCH 31, 1784*

The mud made a suctioning noise with each step Muireall took.

"We have to find a path that does not take us through this muck," John grumbled ahead of her.

According to the map, they were to travel alongside the creek to their right. But with the rains and flooding the day before, the land around it had been turned into a mire of mud and debris. After slipping and sliding down the hillside they had camped on, they had struggled through this mess for over an hour. Muireall's lungs burned and her legs ached. Even Sugar puffed out loud breaths through her nostrils.

John stopped and glanced around, then pointed uphill. "We will move up ground but keep the stream in sight."

Muireall nodded. Surely, the ground on up the hillside would be more solid and easier to traverse. They climbed the uneven terrain, taking a looping path to avoid a couple of fallen trees. Large, muddy bundles of root stuck up from the earth, leaving gaping holes which Muireall gave a wide berth. It was clear they were drawing closer to home, for this land twisted and turned and rose and dipped more than anywhere else on earth, it seemed.

She eyed the second tree as they moved past, her heart beating quickly. The damage from the storm the day before did not bode well for their progress. How she wished John would deem this day an unsuitable day for travel. But she held no expertise on the subject, so she would not question the judgement of her husband. Anyway, drawing nearer to Pitman Station meant being closer to finding her sister. Would Margaret be glad she came, or would Muireall arrive only to find that some tragedy had befallen her sister and brother-in-law?

Muireall pushed the thought to the back of her mind and focused on her steps. The farther they went, the steeper the landscape became, and soon, they were on a precipice, overlooking where the stream fed into a river.

"This does not look right," John muttered to himself as he pulled out the map.

Muireall stood several paces away with her back to a tall oak.

After a moment of pondering and turning the paper this way and that, he pointed to a place on the map where two lines connected. "Right. This is where we are. This is the way."

He picked up Sugar's lead and marched on around the bend. The forest enveloped them, and Muireall could not tell one tree from the next. She grunted as she tripped on a dip in the ground.

John turned and reached for her hand. "Here, walk with me."

Muireall slipped her hand into his, into the strength and assurance he offered. How glad she was to have a helpmate to journey through this land with. When travelling with Margaret and her husband, Muireall had felt she was an outsider among the trio. She and Margaret had worked in harmonious union to save Iain when infection had set in following an injury. But as soon as he recovered, the married two had been closer than ever, and Muireall had been pushed to the background again. She could not blame them, but with her deficit, it seemed the way of life—always in the shadows or wings.

With John, it felt as though she was being coaxed forth from hiding, to bloom in the sunshine. But she could not do so with her secret still hanging between them. Muireall longed for the air to be cleared. For them to truly start their life together. Despite how they leaned upon one another and grew closer each day, it seemed an impenetrable stone wall stood between them, keeping them from truly becoming husband and wife. *Lord, please break down the barriers between us, an' allow us to experience the union that Ye planned for us.* Even as she prayed the prayer, she feared it would mean difficult conversations and even some dark times before they came out on the other side. But God could get them there, could He not?

Slowly, the ground began to slope downhill. But again, they seemed to be in the wash path of the rainwater, for the dead leaves that littered the forest floor were mired in mud. Their steps squished the leaves down into the ground.

After a few minutes of more rough going, John stopped and sighed. "Perhaps we should find a good place to camp for the night and call today a loss."

"I would be amenable to that." Muireall did her best to conceal her smile so as not to appear too eager. But a weight eased from her chest.

John glanced back the way they had come. "We will not attempt returning to the stream. Instead, we will stop at the next place we find that will provide shelter and has water near enough by for us and the horse."

Though that could still mean a great deal of travel, at least there was a silver lining as they moved forward. To their right, the hillside opened up to what appeared to be a massive hole in the earth. Muireall swallowed and kept her feet moving forward, eyes averted from the gaping black pit. But John did not move away. He moved closer. "Is that a cave?"

He approached what appeared to be the edge and peered down into the darkness. Then he knelt, hand on the ground, and leaned farther over the edge to gain a better view. Muireall's fingers tapped along her arm where she hugged herself, and the seconds ticked slowly by as she waited for her husband to return to her side.

At last, John pulled himself upright, and Muireall had only just taken a half step toward him, when suddenly, he was falling. His arms flew into the air as he dropped out of sight. Muireall gasped and darted toward him but was helpless to do anything besides watch as her husband fell into the void. "Nay!"

Muireall dropped to her knees and scrambled to the edge. John's light clothing contrasted with the dark earth below, but there was no movement. Was he unconscious? Or did he lie there with open, unseeing eyes and she simply could not tell? "John!"

When he did not answer, she tried again. This time, her voice came out in a hysterical scream. What would she do if she lost him? How would she ever find her way in the wilderness?

A groan sounded below and her heart leapt. "John?"

"Yeah. I am here." His voice was strained, barely audible. How much pain must he be in?

"Are ye hurt?" Muireall bit her lip while she waited.

"I feel as though someone barreled me over with a wagon, but with the ground as soft as it is, I do not believe anything is broken." John sounded stronger, surer.

Muireall let out a breath of relief. "Are ye certain?"

"Yeah."

Another grunt came from below, and Muireall frowned. But she did not let on that she did not entirely believe John. They could assess his injuries once he was back on higher ground. "Good. Now we just need to figure out how to get ye out of there."

Another bit of silence. "These walls are awfully steep, and there is a cave below. I am not sure that I can climb out."

Muireall glanced around. "Perhaps I can use Sugar to draw ye out with the rope."

"Yes. That should work. Lower one end down, and I will make a loop about my waist. You can tie the other end to the saddle, and she can pull me up. You will just have to coax her to put out the effort."

Muireall eyed the mare next to her. As old and tired as the animal might be, at least she usually did as they asked. This would be different than any request they had made of her, though.

Muireall lowered the rope down and then moved toward the animal. "Can you talk me through this?" She called the question down to John. She could tie off a thread with her eyes closed, but she had never handled a rope.

John did not question her lack of skill and talked her through the steps. Soon, she was positioned next to Sugar's head, asking her to walk on. The horse moved forward until the rope became taut. Then she threw her head in the air and lifted her hind leg where the rope rubbed against it.

"Come on." Muireall put her weight against the lead, but Sugar did not budge. Her leg remained cocked in the air, away from the threat of the rope. Muireall located a tree branch and waved it up and down, but the mare simply eyed her warily. As though she had lost her mind. Muireall sighed.

"John, she will not budge!"

"Do your best." His voice came out strained.

Muireall groaned but turned back to the horse. Doing the only other course of action she could think of, she climbed into the saddle. What had John told her about how to maneuver the animal? She squeezed her legs against Sugar's sides. The mare plodded forward until a cry came from John's direction. Muireall and the mare both froze. "John?"

"I am well," he replied, but it sounded as though it was through gritted teeth.

"Are ye sure?"

"Yeah." Still more of a grunt.

Muireall had to see for herself. What if he was masking an injury to spare her nerves? Or if her inept attempts at pulling him up the side of the ravine were making it worse? She dismounted, scurried around the front of the horse, and made for the ravine. A couple of feet away, her foot caught on a root. As she toppled forward, all she could see was the deep, dark void of the ravine. Over the edge she went, headfirst. A garbled cry from John mixed with hers as she put her hands out in an attempt not to break her neck. Pain shot through her right arm as it took the brunt of the impact.

"Muireall!"

All she could do was lay and whimper as her body absorbed the excruciating sensation. She could not even tell if she was injured besides her arm as she hugged it to herself.

"Muireall. Is it your arm? Are you hurt anywhere else?" A twig crunched underfoot, and John's voice drifted closer.

She did not open her eyes but managed to squeak out an answer. "I dinnae think so."

"Very well. Do not move, but I need to check your arm and see if the bone must be set."

A groan escaped, but Muireall nodded, lips rolled inward in an attempt to restrain any further sound. She had shown enough weakness as it was. She should have seen the root or other hazard that tripped her. Should have saved her husband instead of landing herself in this pit alongside him. Now what were they to do?

# CHAPTER 10

$\mathcal{H}$ow could he have gotten them into this mess? He was supposed to be protecting Muireall, not be the reason they were both down a ravine. John gingerly examined Muireall's arm, his jaw clenching at how her face contorted. Though the bone did not seem to be displaced, he could not rule out a break.

John blew out a breath and glanced around. He easily located a couple of good, straight sticks for her splint and ripped a length from the bottom of his shirt to tie them to her arm. Muireall remained rather stoic throughout the ordeal, whining but once, though he could only imagine the pain she was in. "Let me see if I can get the mare to pull me from here." Or find some other way out. "Then I can make a sling or something to pull you up."

Muireall simply nodded, eyes closed. His heart

twisted at the sight of her lower lip tucked under her teeth.

John limped over to the side of the ravine and clutched the length of rope still attached to his middle. He called out to the mare and twirled it to and fro, but there was no sign of movement from the top. The mare required more convincing than that. John blew out a painful breath. It would be up to him and Muireall to find their way out.

He surveyed the edges of the ravine once more, ignoring the pain that seared through his right ankle and the soreness that stretched across his upper back and around to his left side. No longer did he consider how Muireall could help him, but how he could help her.

One side of the ravine was not quite as steep as the other two, and though it would be difficult with his injuries, it might be possible to make it up. After all, Muireall was counting on him, and he had endured much worse pain before. If he could live through the ordeal he had as a nine-year-old boy, he could face this for the sake of his wife.

Taking hold of a rock, he hoisted himself up the first couple of feet. But when he dug his toe into the soft earth and tried to push farther upward, his foot slipped. He groaned, shoved his boot into the ground again, and pushed. He latched onto a dried plant, but it ripped loose. His nails dug into the rock that held him, but it was no use. He slipped back down the few feet he had gained, his boots squishing into the mud as he landed. A low moan slipped out as agony sliced through his ankle. Still, John gave it one more try with the same result. The ground was simply too muddy and soft. Given another day for the surface to dry, he could be successful. He turned back to Muireall and frowned. He had to be.

For now, though, the ravine led down to a large cave, and it appeared that travel downward would be easier than up. They could camp there for the night and try again tomorrow. That would be better on Muireall, anyway. Then perhaps he could build a travois to bring her up after him. It was midafternoon, and though they would only have the supplies on their bodies, he made sure to keep the most vital materials close at hand. In a leather pouch, he kept flint and steel, as well as a couple strips of jerked meat. Then there was the canteen, knife, and rifle he kept strapped to his body as well as the pistol he had lent Muireall. For a single night, it should be all they needed. The cave was definitely the wiser option. At least for Muireall.

His only concern was the mare. What if she wandered away? Or worse, was stolen, supplies and all? John shuddered at the thought. And though he did not prefer to leave his steed unattended and uncared for, there was little else he could do. The ground was simply too muddy, and both he and Muireall were injured.

He turned and knelt at Muireall's side. Her eyes opened to slits, her jaw still clenched.

"I am going to carry you down to the cave. We will camp there for the night."

Muireall nodded. He moved to the side away from her injured arm and gently scooped her into his arms. She seemed so frail and small, nestled there against his chest. His ankle protested the extra weight, and pain radiated through his ribcage, but he gritted his teeth and moved forward, anyway. It took slow, careful steps, but finally, they were on the solid rock floor of the cave. The temperature dropped several degrees as they moved down into the vast structure, but a fire should easily keep them warm enough.

He lowered Muireall to the ground. "I am sorry that we have nothing to put down on the hard floor."

"'Tis fine." Muireall's voice was small, her pain and tiredness evident. If only he had some way to ease her suffering in their current situation. But the limestone cave held few comforts without their supplies.

John frowned. "I will start a fire. You rest here." Not that she was going anywhere. Still, he pushed himself to gather wood and start a fire as quickly as possible. At least the ravine seemed to catch leaves, sticks, and other debris that made it easy enough to gather what he needed. Only once he had Muireall settled would he consider exploring even the smallest portion of the massive cave. From where he knelt to unload his armful, the structure seemed to stretch on forever.

Soon, the fire crackled as Muireall fell into a fitful sleep. While she was unconscious, the whimpers she had withheld in his presence slipped out and cut through him like a knife.

~

*M*uireall contained a groan as she shifted. Not only was her hip sore from sleeping on the hard stone floor, but the movement shot a new wave of pain through her arm. Her slumber had been restless, and because of her injury, John had not embraced her as they slept. Tears pricked at the backs of her eyes. Though he had remained by her side, without the steady warmth of his body, he seemed a world away. All was cold and hard and uninviting in this stone hideaway.

Muireall closed her eyes and swallowed. She prayed they were able to keep moving today, no matter how terrible the pain. She could withstand it as long as she had hope. And here, all seemed hopeless.

Muireall turned her head toward where John slumbered. But he was not there, only more emptiness. As she glanced the other direction, her gaze landed on where his blurry form stood by the remnants of the fire. "You are awake." Was that a smile on his face?

She pushed herself to a sitting position with her good arm.

"Hey, hey, hey." John came and knelt beside her. "You do not need to do that. You need to rest and heal."

Muireall gave him a pointed look. "We cannae live in this cave while I heal."

John did crack a grin then, but his eyes still held concern.

She rubbed her thumb over his jawline and the dark stubble there in an attempt to comfort him and ease his mind.

"I know. I need a shave," he replied instead.

Muireall gave him a pointed look. "'Tis not what I meant." She moved her touch to the scar on his cheek. "Tell me about this," she urged. The more time she spent with John and the closer they grew, the more she desired to know all there was to know about him. His Adam's apple bobbed, and she was close enough to see, to feel his breath upon her lips.

"You do not want to hear." There was a bite to his voice, a self-loathing she had never heard before.

"I do, John. I want to know all there is about ye."

He closed his eyes and shook his head, his mouth a flat line.

Muireall inhaled deeply. Perhaps it was time she took the first step in forging the gap between them. "If it will make it easier, I need to tell ye somethin' about meself as well." She sighed. "An' ye might wish to leave me behind in this cave after I do."

"What is it?" John settled back on his heels, his voice wary, as though he was bracing for the worst. It did not make what Muireall had to do any easier. But if she wanted her husband to be honest with her, she had to be honest with him.

"I...I am near-sighted. Even as close as ye are to me, ye are blurry. I can only see clearly to right about here." She held her hand up in front of her face. John did not react, so she continued. "I cannae tell ye what is over there." She gestured to a dark mound at the mouth of the cave. Likely, it was mud and leaves, but her eyes could not give her the answer. John still did not respond, and her shoulders sagged.

Finally, he spoke. "You cannot see?"

Muireall shook her head. "Not well."

John stood and began pacing back and forth. "What about your sewing?"

"I know the movements. I can sew with my eyes closed. And if I have a new project or an intricately detailed stitch, I hold the fabric close enough to see."

John let out a loud breath. "And you did not think I needed to know?" He did not give her time to answer before he plowed on. "You lied to me? Omitted an important detail that a man should know before he marries a woman?"

John turned to her as he spat the last question, and it knifed through her chest.

Tears formed in her eyes. "I...I withheld the truth. Aye. I was afraid ye would not want to marry me. I...I can still fulfill all my wifely duties. I can cook an' clean an' sew. Even raise children."

"Raise children! What if they were in danger? How would you know? How could you save them? You set yourself on fire the first night on the trail!"

Muireall recoiled at the volume of John's voice.

He turned with a growl and ran his hands through his hair. Then, he stalked away, into the depths of the cave. Muireall's heart broke as she watched him go, and tears slipped down her cheeks. Only once he was out of earshot did she succumb to the sobs that caused her arm to ache as her shoulders shook. And still, she did her best to remain quiet in the echoing cave.

Her worst fear had come true. She had come to love a man, only to have him resent her once he learned the truth. He thought her to be defective and unworthy— uncapable, even.

What was she to do now?

~

*M*uireall had lied to him, taken him to be a fool. Ignoring the darkness that closed in around him and the pain that reverberated through his ankle with each step, John marched deeper into the cave. So much made sense now. She had caught herself on fire. What he had thought to be a simple accident was actually an indication of her dangerously diminished sight.

How could Muireall possibly believe that she could live a full, normal life? If they had children, how could he entrust their care to her? How could he ever even allow her to venture out of his sight? The woman was a risk to herself and others. She had already proven that. And to think, he had taught her how to shoot his gun. No wonder she could not hit the broadside of a barn.

John's breathing was quick and ragged in the cool air as he pushed farther, his eyes adjusting to the dim interior he had explored the night before. How could she have deceived him so, roping him into a marriage with a broken woman while hiding such a secret from him? He shoved his hand through his hair, his fingertips grazing the leather strap of his eyepatch.

John stopped and sighed.

Sure, he had been made a fool. But so had she. How could he be mad at Muireall for hiding her flaw when he had hidden his own? His shoulders sagged. She did not even know his real name. He had a past that had literally come to haunt them.

Rollinson and Hodges. He had left Muireall alone.

A gunshot split through the air, echoing through the cave. *No!*

John ran back the way he had come.

~

$\mathcal{M}$uireall listened, but she could hear nothing over the pounding of her heart in her ears. Something or someone was in the cave with them. She kept John's pistol aimed in the direction she had fired, but whatever had been rustling around in the leaves near the entrance seemed to have either fled or died. Whichever it was, she prayed the mysterious foe could no longer harm her. At least, not worse than she already was.

"Muireall!"

At John's voice, she whipped around, the pistol still held out before her. But as his familiar form approached, she breathed a sigh of relief and lowered the weapon.

"What happened?" He sounded out of breath as he knelt beside her and eased the gun from her loosened grip.

"There was something rustling about over there." She pointed. Then hesitated before defensively adding, "I could not see what it was to know if it was dangerous."

John sighed, and it was evident what he was thinking. He thought her incompetent, and here she was, proving his point.

"At least you came to no harm. I will check, but it appears you scared whatever it was off." He leaned over and kissed the top of her head before following where she had indicated.

She stared after him. A kiss? Did that mean he had chosen to accept her as she was?

Within moments, John was back by her side, confirming there was no danger. "We should be on our way, though. We should be able to reach Pitman Station today or tomorrow."

"Good." Muireall pushed to standing.

Not a word was spoken between them as John gathered their few supplies. Walking back to the edge of the ravine, his gait appeared stiff, as though he were masking an injury. Muireall frowned. He was allowed to hide that from her, but she could not conceal her own weakness? The intention was different, she supposed. His must be to protect her while hers had only been to protect herself? Still, there was a discussion to be had. If John had chosen to accept her and her deficiency, it rooted a seed of hope for their marriage. But he could apologize for the hurtful words he had spewed.

# CHAPTER 11

*J*ohn stirred water and dried meat in a pot, working to make a broth for Muireall as the day's light slowly slipped away from them. The broth should aid in strengthening his wife, but what would heal her broken heart after she learned his truth? His stomach roiled at the thought.

Muireall sat a few feet away, leaned against a tall maple loaded with whirligigs, her eyes closed as she attempted to rest. But her brow bore wrinkles of pain. With her instruction, he had brewed her some feverfew tea, but it only abated the pain, and the effects could be wearing off.

A growl slipped from John. What kind of monster was he to heap more pain on her when her arm was already broken? But after how he had treated her, he had to apologize and come clean about his own deception. Or else, he feared the guilt would eat him alive, from the inside out.

The rustle of petticoats mixed with the crackling of the fire, and Muireall settled at his side. He stared at the pot to avoid her gaze, but his neck heated under her scrutiny.

John huffed out a breath and withdrew the pot from the fire. Better to get this over with before he combusted. "Muireall, I need to apologize for how I reacted this morning."

Muireall nodded but remained silent.

He wanted to reach out and take her hand but could not bring himself to do so. "I have no right to be angry with you when I have not been honest myself."

"How do ye mean?" Wariness was laced into the words.

John closed his eyes and hung his head. "I am not who you think I am."

"What?" Muireall's breath was shallow, as if the wind had been knocked out of her.

John winced. "I mean, I am. I am still me. But my name is not John. It is Jude." So much like Judas, the man who committed the ultimate betrayal. And the same blood seemed to run through his veins.

"Wh..." The word did not quite come out, but he knew what Muireall was asking. Why had he changed his name? What else was he not telling her?

"I changed my name when I came west. I did not want to be linked to the person I was before."

"Who were ye?" Her voice was so quiet, yet so horrified.

John swallowed. "A no-good man of illegitimate birth."

"Wh-what did ye do?" Muireall's voice shook now, but he could not stop. It was time to lay it all out before her, even if it meant she would be gone from him forever.

"When I was a child, despite not having a father in my life, I tried to be good. Really tried. My mother always told me that just because she made a mistake, it did not make me a bad person. But one day, coming home from school, a handful of the boys ambushed me. They knocked me over the head with a bat." He put a hand to the place, felt the pain ricochet through his brain once more. "Then they pummeled me with rocks while I was down. Told me that I was nothing but a..." He glanced in Muireall's direction. "Well, you know. That because my mother was not married, that I was no better than dirty wash water. That is when I lost the sight in my eye."

A small gasp came from beside him. Muireall lifted her hand as though to reach out to him, then brought it back to her lap.

"After that day, I stopped trying. I realized that if no one would ever see me as more than illegitimate, there was no point in putting out the effort. I kept my head down. And as soon as I was old enough, I took a job at the docks to provide for me and my mother. There, people did not care that I was born out of wedlock as long as I put in a hard day's work. I met Rollinson and Hodges there."

"The men from the fort? One of them made the map."

"Yes. Rollinson. I worked there with them for seven years before my mother passed. It was on her deathbed that she finally revealed my father's name to me. She had lied to me all those years, told me she did not know who he was. Anyway, soon after that, the drinking and thievery caught up with Rollinson and Hodges. They managed to get all three of us fired."

"Ye were a thief an' a drunkard?" Muireall shot to her feet then. The quick movement and the pain it likely caused left her unsteady for a moment, and John followed her. When he offered a steadying hand, though, she backed away, her eyes wide. He was botching this explanation.

"No. No. It was a misunderstanding. I caught the two of them stealing silver cutlery from a crate one day. I tried to stop them, but when the dock master found us, he assumed we were all guilty and would not listen to a word otherwise."

Muireall eyed him, her lips pressed so tightly they could barely be seen.

"That is when I set out to find my father. I thought if I knew who he was, maybe I would finally know who I was." John shook his head. How wrong he had been. Still, he continued the explanation for Muireall's sake.

"All my mother knew was that he had abandoned her to come west, to Kentucky. I saw an opportunity then, to leave my past behind and make a new man of myself while I searched. It almost worked. Until Rollinson and Hodges showed up at Ford Harrod. And I kept my distance at first. But through asking around, I learned that someone had met a man that matched my father's name and description while they were there. I also learned that Rollinson and Hodges had been there and knew the way. And despite his...flaws... Rollinson is the most talented cartographer I know. So I asked him to create the map. You know the rest. I did not want you traveling with them because I knew they had no moral decency. Knew they would not treat you right. But now—"

John stopped and turned, pacing a couple of feet away as she shoved a hand through his hair. Then he faced Muireall again as he dropped the final truth. "Now they are following us."

Muireall sucked in a breath.

"I thought someone was following us, but it did not make any sense, and I never found any evidence, so I thought it was all in my imagination. But then I saw Rollinson when I went hunting. That is why I returned with no game. And I still do not know why they are following us. But they are."

Muireall's face was as pale as a sheet as she stood staring at him with her mouth dropped open. Finally, she whipped toward the trees, her gaze scanning all around. Then she turned on him. "How? How could ye?" She screamed the words, tears streaming down her cheeks. Her chest heaved with rapid breaths.

Pain sliced through his chest. His intention had always been to protect her. And now, with her standing before him, her right arm nestled in the makeshift sling he had prepared before their travel that morning, it was clear. Not only had he broken her physically, but he had robbed her of her peace of mind as well. "I can still protect you. We will be at Pitman Station tomorrow. We will be safe there."

Muireall's blue gaze sliced through him. "Ye! Ye can protect me? I dinnae even know who ye are!"

John's heart plummeted. But he made one more attempt to save the last thread holding his marriage together. "I have never been anyone but myself with you. I have never put on airs or pretended I was playing a part. I only went by a different name."

"An' hid yer motives. An' neglected to tell me that yer comrades are followin' us."

John staggered backward a step. She had hit the nail on the head, and how could he argue with the truth?

Muireall started to storm off but stopped and let out a frustrated growl as she threw her good hand in the air. Likely, she wanted to be anywhere else at the moment. But because of his reprehensible acquaintances, it was not safe for her to leave their camp.

John swiveled back toward the fire, pulled the hat from his head, and threw it into the dirt. He was no better than the dust beneath their feet. His wife was all but a captive in her own marriage. He fell to his knees.

*Oh, Lord, how did I do this?*

~

*M*uireall yawned and scrubbed a hand over her face. The bleak black sky had finally given way to an azure blue, but the heaviness in her chest had not lightened in the least. Sleep had eluded her the night before, for she had either been plagued by the pain in her arm or a flood of hopelessness at any given moment. At this point, she was too exhausted to cry another tear. Nay, somehow she had to fight through the fog in order to move forward with her life.

In the endless thoughts that had sprinted through her mind during the night, she had found one strand of hope. Finding Margaret. Her marriage might be a sham, and she might be ruined for future marriages, but she could endure if only she had her family. To complete the journey alone would be dangerous, to say the least. But they had reached the creek which led to Pitman's Station, and she only needed to follow it to her destination. Someplace she would be safe. Safe from weather and wild animals, safe from nefarious followers, and safe from husbands whose behavior more closely resembled that of a snake.

A tiny prick of regret touched her heart at that thought, but she pushed it away. Not even the memory of him kneeling on the ground, his head in his hands, broken, would soften her heart to John. Nay, not John... Jude. His given name was eerily similar to that of the man who had betrayed Jesus. How fitting.

Muireall carefully maneuvered into a sitting position and cast a glance in Jude's direction. Though he had agreed not to sleep in the same pallet as she, he had insisted that she sleep between him and the fire so he could provide protection should danger strike. But who was to protect her from him?

A frown crimped her mouth, and she rose to her feet. Pain shot through her arm, and she stood still long enough for the wave of dizziness that followed to subside. She could succumb to her injury only once she made it to Pitman Station. For now, she had to be on her way while Jude—and hopefully, Rollinson and Hodges—still slumbered.

Muireall knelt at Jude's side and ever so carefully pulled the map from his pocket. After a moment of examining the markings, she pinpointed their location with her finger, then followed the creek to Pitman Station. After she slipped the paper back into position, she found the pistol and ensured it was loaded. Tucked into her pocket, it weighed heavily as she moved. Last, she draped a canteen over her shoulder and tucked some dried meat into the small pouch at her waist. With supplies in tow, she slipped past Sugar and into the dawn.

~

*J*ude woke with a start. Blinking, he glanced around. The sun loomed above the treetops, and birds chirps nearby. He groaned and pushed upright. He should have risen long ago, but guilt and anguish had kept sleep at bay well into the night. Though only a few feet had separated him from Muireall, it might as well have been a gulf. Jude turned toward her pallet, and his heart seemed to stutter to a stop.

Where was she?

"Muireall?" With no thought to safety, he called her name, his heart slamming against his ribcage. He clamored to his feet, and a paper slipped from his pocket, drifting to the ground. Jude bent, brow furrowed, and picked it up, but it was only the map. He scanned the camp once more. Sugar still rested with her head hung low beside the tree line, yet there was no sign of Muireall.

Had she gone to relieve herself when she awakened and Rollinson and Hodges ambushed her? *Lord, please no.* Jude closed his eyes and swallowed down the urge to retch. If it was money they wanted, they would have brought her into camp to confront him.

He knelt beside her pallet and checked for shoeprints. Crouching, he followed her tracks, crossing one foot over the other until he reached a shuffle of prints beside the packs. Then there were a couple more leading away. Jude sighed and hung his head. Muireall had struck out alone, on foot. With danger hovering, his half-blind wife was unaccompanied in the Kentucky wilderness, utterly defenseless. All because of his foolishness and secrecy.

Jude slammed his fist into the ground, then stood and set to work. There was no time to dwell in the self-pity. He stomped down the dying embers of the campfire, then kicked dirt over it. Quickly, he saddled Sugar and replaced their packs. All loaded and rifle in hand, Jude pushed a foot into the left stirrup and swung into the saddle. The mare's head whipped upward at the sudden presence of his greater weight. Then, as though she sensed his urgency, she picked up a rough, head-bobbing trot. Jude directed her into the woods and toward the creek.

There was no doubt where Muireall had gone—to Pitman Station, to find her sister. He had to locate the woman he loved before Rollinson and Hodges had a chance to take advantage of her vulnerability. He had failed her before, but he could not do so now. Nothing else mattered—nothing else in the world.

# CHAPTER 12

M uireall placed her hand on the massive sycamore tree to her left as she followed the bank up the mound of dirt at its base. The only reason she knew the type of tree was because of the mass of roots that stretched into Sinking Creek beside her. Margaret had pointed one out to her on their journey to the fort. Muireall frowned to consider how cold she had been to her sister after their mother's death. After losing both parents in such a short span of time, she had been embroiled in such a state of grief that her behavior had been repulsive. Fear had also had a tight hold on her, especially once they ventured from the safety of the cabin. When she lost her mother, she had lost the one person who could help her navigate her near-sightedness. The one person who could protect her.

But along the way, Margaret had helped her see that

God was always there, watching and protecting. Even now, she could feel His hand steadying her as she followed the dip back down on the other side of the sycamore. Muireall walked along the dirt bank beside the creek, thankful for the clear path that had been provided. She watched the ground closely for obstructions, stepping over each potential hazard, whether it be a stick or a shadow. Unable to tell the difference, it was better to be safe than sorry. And with no one around to see, she did not have to concern herself with appearing foolish.

'Twas a lonely way to travel, though. As wounded and irate as she was when it came to Jude's deception, she had grown accustomed to his gentle, reassuring presence. The sway of Sugar beneath her. In fact, she had become so used to riding that only an hour's worth of walking had her feet hurting with every step she took. But she could not look back, could not consider those she had left behind.

Nay, she could not concern herself with the absence of someone who could so easily allow lies to roll off his tongue. Even if his intentions were honorable. Muireall shook her head and marched faster, ignoring how her feet ached in the ridiculous shoes women had to endure. Perhaps when she found Margaret, Iain could make her a pair of moccasins as he had done for his wife and child. Margaret's had been crafted for her when her feet had become bruised and bloodied after only a day or two of travel. But even once they arrived at the fort where no other woman would be seen in such, her sister had continued to wear them for their comfort. Her confidence had always been inspiring to Muireall.

When the creek bank turned from dirt to stone, she stopped in her tracks. She glanced from the pale stones to her left to the underbrush to her right. Though the stones themselves could pose a tripping hazard, the ferns and other foliage of the underbrush could hide potential dangers. With a lift of her chin, she clattered out onto the rocks. If there were any varmints nearby, mayhap she would scare them away. A frog did startle her when it jumped from in front of her into the water. Ripples drifted outward from where it broke the surface.

Muireall sighed and continued on a bit farther until a dark swirl at the water's edge caught her attention. Her steps slowed as she eyed what was likely an oddly shaped rock. Forcing air in and out of her lungs, she kept her feet moving forward. Suddenly, the rock uncoiled itself and leapt at her. Muireall fell backward with a scream, her left palm slamming into the rocky earth. She attempted to scramble backward, but her shoes caught in her petticoats. Meanwhile, dark-colored snake coiled for another attack. *Lord, please send it away. Please protect me from this danger.*

For what seemed several minutes, she remained as still as possible, the prayer repeating over and over in her mind as she stared down her forked-tongued foe.

Finally, it slithered away, toward the undergrowth she had avoided.

Muireall released the air from her chest and looked heavenward. *Thank Ye, Lord.*

Muireall dusted her free hand on her petticoats and untangled her feet before she stood. She still hesitated to move. She glanced all around, but the morning seemed quiet now that the snake had departed. But how was she to know for sure? She could be right up on a dangerous situation before she realized what was happening. A thought struck her. It was unconventional and might not last the entire way to the station, but it was better than nothing.

Kneeling, she held the flap on her bag open with her restricted hand while she used the other to scoop rocks inside. Before she continued on, she tossed a small stone ahead of her. She continued across the rocky bank without incident, then stepped up onto where roots provided natural steps to solid ground. The next stone she threw startled a small bird from its hiding.

A grin stretched her face. Her idea was working. And for once, she was proving herself completely capable in the face of her weakness.

*A*s Muireall stepped into the clearing where Pitman Station stood, her smile slipped from her face. An eerie silence filled the air. No words carried on the wind, being shared with family members or neighbors. There were no stirrings of farm animals milling about. Not even a crow squawking overhead. Muireall stopped, surveying for signs of life. Yet she found none.

Slowly, she approached the station master's home. William Pitman and his wife, Sallie, had been welcoming when she, Margaret, and Iain had stopped on their way to the fort. What she would not give for a friendly face at this moment. But the building was in a state of disrepair, vines and tall grasses encroaching on all sides of the cabin. Even a maple sapling poked out at her as she approached the door.

Muireall knocked, but there was no answer. Deep within, she knew the reason why. Still, she knocked again, harder. It could not be. "Hello," she called through the thick wood. She turned and glanced around, her heart picking up its pace.

She spun and hammered her fist against the door. "Hello!"

When there was still no answer, Muireall pushed the door. It did not budge. After she shoved her good shoulder into it, it finally creaked open, the hinges having gathered rust. Inside, Muireall's hand dropped to her side, and her shoulders sagged. Empty darkness greeted her. She moved through the interior in a daze, finding only dust and cobwebs.

*Nay. Nay, this cannae be happenin'.* Muireall squeezed her eyes shut.

The station had been abandoned and quite some time ago, at that. There was no one to aid her in locating her sister, no one to protect her from the danger that lurked on her tail, and no one to offer a comforting word or warm cup of tea when pain throbbed through her arm, reminding her of the injury that would never see physician care on this desolate frontier. Muireall crumpled in a heap on the floor, cradling her broken arm as tears flowed down her face. Great sobs erupted from her chest with no one to hear her cries. "Lord, why?"

She was hopelessly alone, her marriage in ruins. There seemed no way out of the long, dark tunnel that was her circumstances. What was she to do now? She could not attempt to travel on to her sister on her own. With no sense of direction and no way to tell one tree from the next, she would find herself lost in the wilderness. If she stayed in the shelter of the station, she would run out of supplies with no way to replace them. And she could not go back to Jude. Could she?

The thought seemed imprudent. After all, what man would take his wife back after she had walked out on him? But the more she considered it, the more peace seeped into her soul, and her tears slowed. Even if Jude would not have her as his wife after her rash behavior of the morning, perhaps he would at least see to her safety before moving along. As livid and despairing as she had been at the disclosure of his deceit, he had proved trustworthy in every other aspect in the time she had known him. After all, he had only ever had her safety in mind. Perhaps, as he claimed, she could trust in him...if he would have her.

Muireall rose and left the dusty building, returning to the sunshine outside. After taking a deep breath of the fresh air, she set off. She had already made this journey alone once this morning. She could do it again. And if her husband proved to be the man she thought him to be, she would only need to make it as far as Jude. Likely, even if he had been infuriated when he realized her missing, he would have set out in search of her. And she had made it no secret where she was headed.

But as Muireall delved deeper back into the woods, her determination waned. The sun on the trees cast long shadows that stretched out toward her ominously, and she could not shake the sensation of being watched. With every rustle of a bush or chatter of a squirrel, she whipped toward the sound while her feet continued to carry her forward, away from possible threats. Muireall felt in her pocket for the pistol, wrapping her fingers around the smooth wooden handle. Then, straightening her spine, she focused her attention ahead and pushed on. There was no sense in this. She was only on edge because of Jude's revelation about Rollinson and Hodges trailing them.

But it was more than a revelation. It was the truth.

Muireall stopped. She closed her eyes against the shiver that tingled up her spine. What had she gotten herself into? What if she ran into Rollinson and Hodges before she found Jude? Would it be safer for her to go back to the station and wait for Jude there? Her shoulders drooped as she wrestled with indecision. She spun and took a step back in the direction she had come but halted before she could go any farther. Where was the confident Muireall of the morning who had struck off on her own? She could do this.

With God, all was possible. To remind herself, as she walked, she spoke aloud the passage that had helped her face her fears when she journeyed north with her sister. When, for the first time since their parents had passed, she had learned to hand over her cares to the Lord and trust in His protection. "'Yea, though I walk through the valley of the shadow of death, I will fear no evil: for thou art with me; thy rod and thy staff they comfort me.'"

With each step, the tension in her shoulders eased.

Above her, a tree branch creaked. Muireall swallowed but kept her feet moving. Until several more creaks and pops followed. She whirled toward the sounds in time for a scream to tear from her chest.

Rollinson came crashing down upon her from the treetops. She cried out as they slammed into the ground and pain ripped through her arm. While her attacker recovered, so did she, and she used her good arm to scrabble free from his entanglement. Before she could gain her footing, though, he grabbed her legs and pulled her back toward him.

Muireall kicked and struggled with all her might, but her arm had her at a disadvantage. He leaned over her, his fingers pressing into the top of her injured arm as he pushed both her upper arms to the ground. Her petticoats entrapped her legs and kept her blows from reaching her captor. Tears rolled down her cheeks.

"Aw, the precious little wife is injured." He sneered as he glanced from her arm to her face.

Muireall gritted her teeth and squirmed, reaching with her left hand. Her fingertips grazed the fabric of her skirt. If only she could get to the pistol.

Rollinson smashed his face against hers. His rancid breath filled her senses, and she twisted her head to get away. He moved his hand from her injured arm to her jaw, forcing her face forward. A whimper slipped free. She squeezed both her eyes and her mouth shut. A knee pressed on her free hand, keeping it from her pocket and the gun, and her tears came with new force. *Lord, please, save me from this.*

～

"*R*ollinson!" Jude's voice boomed across the forest before he fired off a warning shot.

A calm, malicious grin spread across the blonde's weathered face as he turned toward Jude.

"Look who decided to join us." The man stood, leaving Muireall to crawl away, just as Jude had hoped. But where was Hodges? "Thought you had done let this little filly run away without you. Thought somebody should keep her warm, take care of her." Rollinson's tone told Jude that he would do anything but as he said.

"You touch my wife again and the next bullet will go through you." Jude swallowed. He did not wish to take the man's life, but he would protect his wife.

A shot echoed through the trees nearly the same time as pain ripped through his left arm. The rifle fell from his grasp. Rollinson laughed, and Hodges came walking out of the trees. On his knees, Jude ignored the pain and lifted the rifle, facing off with Hodges. His heartbeat pounded through both his head and his arm.

"We have you, Jude. Now give us our map," Hodges demanded.

Jude kept his rifle trained on the man, but he glanced from Hodges to Rollinson and back. "Map? You want the map back?"

"Yes. Rollinson gave you the wrong one," the redhead grumbled. "It has a key on it to—"

"Hodges!" Rollinson's voice stopped the man from spilling their secret, and Hodges turned wide eyes upon his comrade.

With a window open, Jude dropped his gun and shoved off the ground with his good foot, launching himself at Hodges's middle. The burly man's own rifle fell to the earth as Jude's body impacted his. Pain seared through Jude's ribs. When they hit the ground, Jude lodged his right forearm over Hodges's windpipe. Anything to gain the advantage and stop the varmint from rising again. A beefy arm flew through the arm and slammed into the side of his head, though, causing his body to go limp and blackness to flash before his eyes.

He thought he heard Muireall scream, "no," but even sounds were muffled temporarily as his brain fought to catch up with what was happening. Before he could react, Hodges landed a punch right where his ribs were likely already broken. Jude's body folded in pain. Hodges shoved him to the side and stood, recovering his weapon. A groan escaped as Jude once again found himself staring down the long barrel of the rifle.

"Give us the map."

Jude frowned and reached for his pocket. Perhaps he should have waved the map like a white flag rather than rushing Hodges. But his fingers found no folds of paper where the map usually sat. Jude's heart plummeted as he shoved his hand into the pocket. Still, he found nothing. No, it could not be. Frantically, he searched his body. Ignoring the weapon aimed at him, he glanced all around. Surely, it had been dislodged from its safe hiding spot during the struggle. But there was only green earth surrounding them.

Jude sat up and glanced behind him. "I had it. It was right here. It must have fallen out."

"Sure, it did." Hodges's slow words were dripping with sarcasm.

"It was!" Jude glanced around. His left arm throbbed, but he searched the grass with his right hand. It had to be there somewhere.

"I think you are lying." Beyond Hodges, Rollinson weighed into the discussion. "And I think that this little filly over here can convince you to tell the truth." He had Muireall standing now, her injured arm in his grasp, and he jerked her toward him, a knife held up to her face. A whimper escaped from Muireall as she squeezed her eyes shut and Jude's chest constricted.

"He is tellin' the truth. I put the map back in his pocket this mornin' meself." Her eyes popped open, and her face crumpled in anguish. "Oh, Jude, this is me fault. It fell out 'cause of me."

Jude started to stand, but Hodges pressed the rifle into his shoulder, reminding him that he was still at their mercy. "No, Muireall. The map did fall out this morning. But I put it back." It was an attempt to ease his wife's mind, but in that moment, Jude realized the truth. Once again, the trouble they were in was his fault.

He had hurriedly shoved the map back in place and left camp in a flurry. Likely, it fell out along the way, and he did not notice in his haste to reach Muireall. Jude set his jaw and turned to Rollinson. He would make this right one way or another. "I have looked at the map countless times. Whatever you need, I will do it. I will be your map."

"Nay!" When Muireall took a step toward Jude, Rollinson jerked her back.

"Oh, he is not going anywhere without you, darlin'. We need some insurance that he will not lead us astray."

Jude bristled. "No, you do not. You can trust me."

Rollinson let out a sinister laugh. "Trust you? I do not know what kind of scheme you are a runnin' callin' yourself John, but I would not trust you as far as I could throw you. If it were not for you, we would still have our positions at the docks where we had prime access to whatever loot we wanted. We had it made there, but because you thought yourself high and mighty, we got caught. If you hadn't been arguing with us that day, the dock master never would have taken notice. He never did."

Hodges grunted his agreement from near Jude's shoulder.

"Fine. What do you want?"

"You know where the cross was marked on the map?" Rollinson walked closer, Muireall in tow.

Jude's brows bunched together. The symbol had been located near Pitman Station. "Yes. I thought it was a church."

Another cold laugh from Rollinson. "That is exactly what he wanted you to think."

A sinking feeling wrapped itself around Jude, and cotton seemed to lodge in his throat. "Who?"

# CHAPTER 13

"Your father."

It was as though Jude had been bowled over by an ocean wave back in the Virginia harbor and was fighting for the surface. "My..."

"Father. Yes, it appears you come by your skills at deception honestly, Jude. Now, walk and talk." Rollinson gestured him forward with his knife but did not release his hold on Muireall's arm. Somehow, Jude convinced his feet to move against the quicksand that seemed to hold them in place. Each movement seemed as though he was slogging through mud.

"Where is Sugar?" Muireall's voice broke through the haze.

Jude stopped and turned, glancing between Hodges and Rollinson. There was no way they would allow him to go get the horse, but he could not leave the faithful mare alone either. "She is just over that rise." He lifted his chin toward where the land rose several yards away. On the other side, the earth dipped downward, and it had provided the perfect cover for him to ambush these men. If only it had worked as well as he planned.

Finally, Rollinson released Muireall, and in an instant, she was by Jude's side. Rollinson sheathed his knife and took the rifle from Hodges. "Go fetch the nag."

Muireall shot a glare at their oppressor at his insult to their mare. "We are not goin' anywhere until ye let me tend this wound." Her touch was light against his arm, and he ventured a glance at the injury he had ignored before now. Blood stained over a third of his sleeve. No wonder he was in such a fog. Still, he placed his hand over Muireall's.

"Eh, he will be fine." Rollinson echoed his thoughts.

Muireall turned blue eyes filled with fire upon the man. "He will be of no help to ye if he bleeds to death. Now, ye will either let me tend to him, or we will not be a goin' anywhere."

Rollinson eyed her warily. "Suit yourself." He gestured with the gun for them to sit on the ground.

Jude allowed himself to sink to the earth with Muireall at his side. He could not bear to look into her concerned gaze, so he laid against the cool grass and closed his eyes.

What hand did his father play in all of this? And was Jude really so much like a man he had never met? It sure seemed that, despite all his good intentions, he was destined to ruin Muireall's life as his father had ruined his mother's.

~

*M*uireall brushed her fingers over the pale skin of Jude's cheek. Was it the loss of blood that created his pallor, or the revelation that his father had some part in all of this? In a way, despite his father having left his mother unwed and with child, it seemed that Jude had held him on a pedestal. Mayhap he had latched onto an unfounded belief that the man had some reason for his actions that would redeem his character. And if the father's character were redeemed, then so would the son's be?

Though it seemed illogical, she could not fault her husband for gasping onto what hope he could. His father had been the missing piece to the puzzle of his life, but now that puzzle piece might turn out to be warped and blackened. Muireall took a deep breath as Hodges approached with Sugar. *Lord, please protect me husband from the wounds he has sustained an' will sustain yet today. Both those seen an' unseen.*

"I need the medical kit from that pack there." She pointed at the blurred shapes behind the saddle. "The top one there on the left." While Hodges fetched the leather pouch for her, she tore her husband's ripped shirt open wider. The bullet had left a sizeable gash right below the elbow, and blood still seeped from the opening. "This is gonna hurt," she warned Jude as she pulled the brown bottle of iodine from the pouch. Her husband's foresight in carrying a medical kit with them could very well save his own life.

"Hurry up. Just pour some of that on there and get moving." Rollinson waved his arm at the bottle, then out at the woods.

Muireall shot him another glare. The pistol was burning a hole in the pocket of her petticoats, but she would wait until the right moment to put it from hiding. And this was not the moment. "The wound needs to be closed, or he will die before he can take ye where ye want to go. I need me sewin' kit from the same pack." Though the situation was not quite as dire as she made it seem, it was imperative that she sew the flesh closed to prevent further blood loss.

Rollinson let out a huff before he motioned for Hodges to retrieve her supplies.

Muireall laid a hand on Jude's chest, and finally, he peered up at her. "This will hurt," she warned.

He watched her without a word, until Hodges dropped her sewing kit on the ground beside her. Then Jude nodded and gave her hand a squeeze.

Thanks to her deft skills with needle and a thread, her task was completed in a few short minutes, and they were on their way.

Jude gripped her hand as they led the way ahead of Rollinson and Hodges. Besides their footfalls, the only sound was the gurgle of Sinking Creek to their left. But the tension in the air was palpable, and time ticked slowly by as they made the trek back to Pitman Station.

Outside the abandoned station master's home, Jude released her hand and closed his eyes, likely picturing the map in his mind. Then he turned and surveyed their surroundings. To her, the trees on the horizon just created a jagged green contrast to the light-blue sky.

"There." Jude pointed before he charged ahead, into the tall grass of the meadow between them and the tree line. "So are you going to tell me what we are searching for if it is not a church?" He threw the question back to Rollinson.

"What do you think it is?"

"Money. That and whiskey were the only things that ever seemed to motivate you."

Muireall glanced at the relentless green landscape as she fought through wave upon wave of grass that reached to her knees. Where were they ever supposed to find money in the middle of nowhere?

"More than any one man could ever need."

Muireall shook her head. Greed did strange things to a man.

"Hush, Hodges." Rollinson hit the shorter man over the back of the head with the stock of the rifle.

Muireall paused, her fingers itching for the pistol. Perhaps getting the men talking could work in their favor?

"What does that have to do with Jude's father?" She

glanced toward her husband but could not detect a visible reaction. He certainly did not slow his steps.

The laugh that slipped from Rollinson sent prickles up the back of her neck despite the sun shining overhead. *Lord, please protect us from these men. Help us find a way out of this mess.* "The old man posed as a traveling man of the cloth. Always wore all black with that white band at his neck. Not a person thought twice about allowing him into their homes. Even when their valuables went missing, they would not suspect him for a moment."

"What does that have to do with us now?" Jude spoke up, his tone suspicious.

"A couple miles west of Pitman Station is where he was last said to be seen alive. Rumor is, he buried all his riches under a rock outside his cabin. And when the natives came through a few years ago, they took him but left the money."

Muireall whipped toward Rollinson at the same time as Jude. Her hands went to her hips while her husbands' formed fists at his sides. "Ye mean to tell me ye knew all along the station was abandoned?"

"And that you knew my father was already dead, but you sent us on this wild goose chase just so we could lead you to your money?" Jude took a step forward but stopped when the rifle was raised to point at his chest.

"Ha! I did not need you to lead me here. My map showed exactly where we needed to go. Yours was supposed to send you to the middle of nowhere. But pea brain over here managed to mix them up."

"Who are you calling pea brain?" Hodges gave the man a shove.

Rollinson stumbled a step before he turned on him. With the rifle dropped to his side, he loomed over the shorter man. "You, idiot. All you have done on this entire trip is get in the way."

Now was her moment. Muireall whisked the pistol from her pocket and leveled it, one-handed, at Rollinson's chest. "Enough!"

Silence fell over the group as Hodges and Rollinson directed their attention to her. A smile that even she could tell was sinister stretched across Rollinson's face. "Aw, you wouldn't shoot a man, now, would you?"

"Aye. I would." The venom in Muireall's voice seemed to break through Rollinson's confidence, for his grin slipped from its place, and he held his free hand up. The rifle still hung at his side, though.

Hodges turned to Rollinson. "Ah, she ain't really going to shoot you."

Muireall's teeth pressed together. She lowered the gun and pulled the trigger, then immediately cocked the hammer back.

"She's crazy," Hodges howled. "She got my foot. She got my foot." The burly man proceeded to hop on one foot as he reached for the other one.

"Ow, that's *my* foot, you fool," Rollinson protested

when he landed on him. He shoved at Hodges's thick torso.

Jude used that moment to plow the taller man over. The rifle dropped from his grip as the impact took his lanky frame to the ground. Jude scrambled from atop him and recovered the weapon. He whipped it toward Rollinson. "This is over. Now. You two will do as we say and no one else will be hurt." His voice spoke undeniable authority over the situation.

Hodges stopped his wild dance and nodded rapidly. Rollinson grumbled his assent.

"Good. Both of you, on your knees." Jude stood and motioned for Hodges to join Rollinson on the ground. Once they had both done as he instructed, he glanced in her direction. "Muireall, can you fetch some rope from the packs?"

Muireall dipped her chin in a quick nod. She eased the hammer back down on the pistol and slipped the weapon into her pocket, then moved over to Sugar's side. Despite all the commotion, the mare grazed contentedly only a couple paces away from where Rollinson had dropped her reins to argue with his comrade.

"'Pride goeth before destruction, and an haughty spirit before a fall,'" she whispered with a shake of her head. Rollinson was evidently a man capable of absolutely anything, but his mean spirit had been his downfall. How did a man with such potential become so twisted? She puzzled the thought over as she fished the rope from their packs. Then she maneuvered her way through the tall grass to Jude's side. Right where she belonged.

"Can you tie them up?" Jude raised his brow and tilted his head in the direction of their captives. Admiration shone in his eyes, and the corners of his mouth tipped up on a smile.

"Aye. A knot I can handle." She may not be used to tying a rope around a person or a saddle, but tying something off that was not intended to come undone? She had plenty of practice with that.

Both men grumbled about how tight she tied their wrists, but Muireall ignored their complaints. Once they were secured, Jude checked the ropes and hauled them to their feet.

While keeping his gun at the ready, he leaned forward to peer at the foot Hodges had been so worried about. "You shot through the toe of his boot!"

"Barely missed my foot," the large man complained.

Now that the danger had passed, she and Jude shared a chuckle at Hodges's antics. Jude slipped an arm around her waist and pressed a kiss to her forehead, an act she prayed boded well for their future.

"Perhaps I should stop tryin' to aim. Then I might actually hit me target."

"If that is what works, I am all for it." He beamed down at her before he helped her into the saddle and ordered Rollinson and Hodges forward, back to the station.

Muireall breathed a sigh of relief as she asked Sugar to walk on. Tension that had been there since she left the station hours before eased from her shoulders. A breeze picked up stray strands of her hair and brushed them against her cheeks as she settled into the steady rhythm of her horse's plodding gait. Despite how she had attempted to convince herself that morning, it was truly better to have those she cherished alongside her on the journey rather than to attempt it on her own. And now, with Hodges and Rollinson no longer a threat, the tables had turned once again. This time, in their favor.

# CHAPTER 14

"Come, take a walk with me outside." John appeared at Muireall's side and placed a hand at her elbow. She took the hand he offered to help her up and followed closely behind him as they left their charges inside the station master's old home. The bright afternoon sun had finally lowered to just over the tree line on the western horizon. But as much as she longed for an end to this endless day, she did not look forward to the night.

"What are we goin' to do with them?" Muireall whispered the question as Jude pulled the door shut behind them.

He sighed. "I am not quite sure. There is no one in this area to enforce law and order, and we cannot leave them tied up forever."

A chill ran up Muireall's spine, and she stepped closer to Jude. The thought of those men loose again...

still, she did not enjoy sharing the cabin with them either.

Jude rubbed the top of her arm. "I know. But I will not let them harm you ever again."

She turned wide eyes upon her husband at the sound of those adamant words. "Ye forgive me?"

"Forgive you? Whatever for?"

In contrast to his raised brows, hers lowered. "For leavin' ye."

Jude gave her a pointed look and took her hand into his. "You were angry. And rightfully so. Anyway, I walked away myself in the cave. Remember?" He smiled and squeezed her hand. "But the real question is, do you forgive me for betraying your trust?"

Muireall leaned into him and pushed onto her toes to kiss his cheek. "Of course, I do." It seemed, after all, that they had both learned a great deal about honesty over the past couple of days. How different would their circumstances be now if they had only been truthful with one another from the beginning?

Muireall sighed and dropped her head against Jude's chest. "There is one more thing that I need to be honest with ye about."

"There is?" The words rumbled through his ribs and against her forehead.

"Aye. The reason I wanted to find me sister is 'cause I was havin' the same nightmare over an' over. She was walkin' through the woods, an' a man attacked her."

Jude pulled back and looked into her face. "And you were concerned about her safety."

Muireall nodded as emotions from the assault and the past few weeks flooded through her. Tears rolled down her cheeks. "The nightmares would not stop, an' there was this constant feelin' that somethin' bad was to happen. When Petunia passed an' didna need me anymore...." She squeezed her eyes shut. "But it happened exactly how it happened today when Rollinson leapt from that tree. Somehow, the dreams were tellin' me what was to happen to me, not to her."

Jude pulled her close and rubbed her hair. "Shhh. All is well now. You are safe. I do not know what we will do, but they will never hurt you again. Not if I have anything to do with it."

Muireall turned her face to his. "Ye mean, ye dinnae think I should be institutionalized?"

Jude let out a hearty chuckle that she could feel in her bones and brought a smile to her face. "No, darlin', I do not think you are crazed. There are some things in life which we simply cannot explain." He paused. "Such as this, right now, with you in my arms. Who would have thought that I of all people could find someone to care for me?"

The love that reflected in his face, even with one eye, was enough to steal her breath away. "Jude, I more than care for ye." She rubbed her thumb over the bandage on his arm. "I dinnae know what I would have done if somethin' had happened to ye. An' not 'cause I would have been hopelessly lost on me own. I truly am sorry for leavin' ye."

"Do not give it another thought."

Jude kissed her then. His lips pressed to hers in a gesture that told that all was forgotten between them, and finally, they could move forward. Muireall melted into the embrace, into the strength of her husband and all that the kiss promised. When he pulled back, a smile lifted her cheeks.

"And if you still wish to find your sister," he said, "I will be more than glad to help you do so."

"What about yer father's place? Do ye wish to see it?"

Jude frowned and glanced across the meadow, in the direction they had headed earlier. "That man was never my father. He was only some swindler who pulled the wool over my mother's eyes. I want nothing to do with his ill-gotten worldly goods. I have a heavenly Father and I have you, and that is all I need." The corners of his mouth tipped up. "I only want to continue on the journey He has for us, whatever it is."

Muireall leaned into him, nestling her head against his shoulder. "Me too." In her heart, she knew that meant finding her sister and embracing family in the middle of this wilderness. But suddenly, she was not scared of the prospect. Instead, only joy and hope abounded as she looked out across the landscape, bathed in light but otherwise indistinguishable.

~

APRIL 3, 1784

"If either of you show your face around here again, we will not be so forgiving."

Rollinson shot Jude a glare but turned and walked away.

"You will not see us again," Hodges reassured him.

Jude gave the man a nod and stepped back beside his wife. He whispered a silent prayer for the men he and Muireall had decided to send on their way with a small pack of supplies and a knife. Though there was no perfect solution, it seemed the right thing to do. Keeping their gun minimized the risk of an ambush, and it seemed inhumane to take any course of action besides letting them go free. Although, Jude had been sorely attempted to leave them tied up with only a knife left somewhere out of reach. After all, they had attacked his wife.

Muireall slipped her hand into his and leaned against him as the two troublemakers went on their way. "How are we to be sure that they will not return?"

Jude smiled down at her. "If they do, it will be to find that treasure, not us. Especially since they know we will not hesitate to shoot. We can only pray they choose to return to the fort and turn their lives around."

Muireall nodded, and he held Sugar's reins while she mounted. Between nervousness at sleeping so close to the men who had attacked her and eagerness to reach her sister, it was clear she had barely slept the night before. But the dark rims under her eyes were the only indication, for she sat tall, her focus fixed on the direction in which he led the mare.

It was a miracle to behold, how God had brought them together and seen them through the past ten days, even through their own follies and sins. He supposed it was much like the grace they had shown Rollinson and Hodges. And after all the grace Jude had received in his life, he was not sure he could do anything but offer it in return.

~

*A*head of Muireall, Jude stopped as he topped the rise. He turned to her, a broad grin evident on his face, even in spite of her diminished sight. She drew in a quick breath and slipped from the saddle as fast as she could with her layers of petticoats and broken arm.

As she joined her husband, her hand flew to her mouth. There, at the bottom of the valley, was a cabin with what appeared to be two dark-headed adults and two children out in the clearing. From the distance, they were only specks. But in her heart, she knew. She took off downhill as fast as she could safely manage, guarding her arm in case she fell.

"Muireall," John called after her, his voice laced with the sound of laughter.

Muireall could not help the grin that caused her own cheeks to ache as she scurried forth.

As soon as she broke into the clearing where the home sat, she called out to her sister. "Margaret!" Everyone whipped toward the crazed person who ran toward them. But one woman started running in her direction, a hand going to her mouth.

Muireall's feet did not stop until she crashed into her sister. She wrapped her good arm around the body that she knew so well and wept. Though her sister's figure had filled out with motherhood, there was an unmistakable comfort and familiarity in her hug.

After a few moments, Margaret pulled back and held her at arm's length. Her eyes were misted and her brown hair braided over her shoulder. "What happened? How did ye find us?"

Muireall smiled and swiped her own tears away. "'Tis a long story. Me arm is broken, but I am well, an' it will heal."

"Broken?" Margaret's eyes widened, and she looked Muireall over. But then her gaze softened. "Ye are well, truly?"

Muireall nodded, and her tears welled again. "Never better."

"That is good to hear." Iain's familiar voice drifted to her as he approached, a toddler in tow and a young boy at his side, both spitting images of their father with black hair and bright blue eyes.

She offered them all a smile before she turned back to her sister. "My, how ye have been blessed."

Margaret dropped her hands down to Muireall's and gave them a squeeze. "Verra," she replied in a quiet voice, tight with emotion. "An' ye?" She tipped her head to indicate behind Muireall.

She turned to find Jude and Sugar just entering the clearing. Her husband had convinced the mare into a choppy trot with him running alongside her as they attempted to catch up. Both were out of breath as they approached.

"Margaret, this is me husband, Jude."

Her sister's eyebrows shot up, but her smile was wide and genuine.

Jude swept his hat from his head and extended his hand. "It is nice to meet you, ma'am. Your sister has been very much looking forward to this reunion."

Muireall's heart was about to burst with happiness as she took in their joyful, smiling faces. Four years ago, she never would have imagined that this would be the happiest moment of her life, here, back in the wilderness. It did not matter that she could not see beyond Jude's strong profile or Margaret's broad grin, for she was surrounded by loved ones who would walk with her on her journey. And with them by her side, and the Holy Spirit in her heart, she was home.

# EPILOGUE

*MAY 18, 1784*

*A*longside Margaret, Muireall gathered dishes and returned them to the basket in which they had carried the food and supplies for their picnic. Warm sunshine bathed them while a gentle breeze kissed their faces. Muireall paused and closed her eyes, releasing a contented sigh. Now full of green leaves, the trees of the forest offered their hushed whispers while a cardinal chirped its tell-tale "tweet" from a safe distance.

Deep chuckles drew her from her reverie, and she turned to where Jude and Iain played mock sword-fight with the boys with long sticks they had scavenged up. Muireall smiled. "They are so precious," she told her sister for what was probably the millionth time in the last month and a half.

"That they are." Margaret gave her usual contented reply, as she, too, leaned back and watched the men and boys play.

Muireall settled in next to her, testing her arm as she leaned on it. Though the bone had mended, the muscles protested the stretching after their time of confinement.

Once again, she closed her eyes and turned her face heavenward. *Thank Ye, Lord, for the blessin' of family. An' for gettin' us here today, all together, Margaret's family an' me own. I only pray that Ye bless ours as Ye have hers.*

A shadow fell over Muireall, and she opened her eyes to find her husband smiling down at her. He pulled his hat from his head and tossed it to the side as he settled beside her. He leaned close. "I suppose it could not hurt to have a couple of young 'uns of our own runnin' around."

Muireall planted a kiss on his cheek. "I believe ye read me mind." She nestled into his strong, if sweaty, embrace and relaxed into the joy and peace of the moment.

"Hey." Jude nudged her, coaxing her attention to his face. "I love you."

Muireall grinned. "I love ye too."

Finally, after years of searching, she had no fear of the future and what it might hold. Over and over, the Lord had seen her through the unimaginable. And now, she was surrounded by family who could help her through whatever life threw her way. That, it seemed, was the greatest blessing. For now that the truth was in the open, she had the support she needed. No longer did she have to wander through the darkness alone.

Did you enjoy this book? We hope so!
**Would you take a quick minute to leave a review
where you purchased the book?**
It doesn't have to be long. Just a sentence or two telling
what you liked about the story!

Receive a FREE ebook and get updates when new Wild
Heart books release: https://wildheartbooks.org/
newsletter

# AUTHOR'S NOTE

Thank you for joining me for Muireall and Jude's story. I hope you adored every moment. This one was interesting for me, as I, too, am near-sighted. In many ways, I enjoyed considering what life would be like for me in a time when corrective eyewear was not commonplace, especially on the frontier.

If you have stayed with me for the duration of the Frontier Hearts series, I cannot thank you enough for your support. Without the support of my readers, there is no way I could continue doing what I do.

If you wish to continue following my writing, please join us in The Reader's Nest on Facebook. This series may be over, but there is more to come, and in this place, you can connect with other readers and help contribute to my stories! I look forward to seeing you there.

# ABOUT THE AUTHOR

Andrea Byrd is a Christian wife and mom located in rural Kentucky, who loves to spend time with her family in the great outdoors, one with nature. Often described as having been born outside her time, she has a deep affinity for an old-fashioned, natural lifestyle.

With a degree in Equine Health & Rehabilitation gathering dust and a full-time job tethering her to a desk eight hours a day, Andrea decided it was time to show both herself and her children that it is truly possible to make your dreams come true. Now with over 1,000 contemporary Christian romance novellas sold, Andrea is pursuing her passion of writing faith-filled romance woven with a thread of true history.

# Want More?

If you love historical romance, check out the other Wild Heart books!

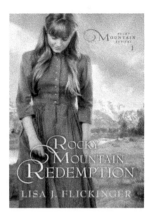

*Rocky Mountain Redemption by Lisa J. Flickinger*

**She's a debutante with broken dreams...He's a preacher with an unsavory past...Both want to bury their secrets...**

Charles Bailey's life has done a complete turnaround. He may still be a logging crew foreman, and he may still have a past that would make a godly man weep, but he's also a man with a changed heart and a mission to serve as pastor to a small logging community. If only walking the narrow path weren't so difficult. The last thing he needs is the temptation of the vulnerable—and beautiful—new cook's assistant. It's clear she needs a friend, but anything more than that is completely off-limits...

Disgraced and grieving, Isabelle Franklin is packed off to work in a logging camp's kitchen in the Rocky Mountains. Though feeding a crew of barbaric lumberjacks can't be further from her life's dream, she finds a small measure of solace in the beauty of the land. And in the unexpected kindness of the camp's foreman, who's broad shoulders and gentle eyes make her feel...almost safe. Is it too much to hope that her unspeakable past can stay buried?

But not even the great Rocky Mountains can hide a person's secrets forever—not when God means to bring them to light. When all the gritty truth is laid bare, two hearts are forced to decide what they truly believe about God's amazing grace.

∼

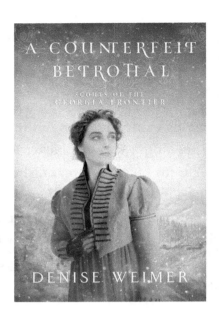

*A Counterfeit Betrothal by Denise Weimer*

**A frontier scout, a healing widow, and a desperate fight for peace.**

At the farthest Georgia outpost this side of hostile Creek Territory in 1813, Jared Lockridge serves his country as a scout to redeem his father's botched heritage. If he can help secure peace against Indians allied to the British, he can bring his betrothed to the home he's building and open his cabinetry shop. Then he comes across a burning cabin and a traumatized woman just widowed by a fatal shot.

Freed from a cruel marriage, Esther Andrews agrees to winter at the Lockridge homestead to help Jared's pregnant sister-in-law. Lame in one foot, Esther has always known she is secondhand goods, but the gentle carpenter-turned-scout draws her heart with as much skill as he creates furniture from wood. His family's love offers hope even as violence erupts along the frontier—and Jared's investigation into local incidents brings danger to their doorstep. Yet how could Esther ever hope a loyal man like Jared would choose her over a fine lady?

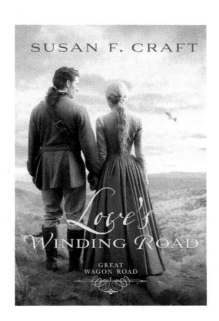

*Love's Winding Road by Susan F. Craft*

*They were forced into this marriage of convenience, but there's more at stake than their hearts on this wagon train through the mountain wilderness.*

When Rose Jackson and her Irish immigrant family join a wagon train headed for a new life in South Carolina, the last thing she expects is to fall for the half-Cherokee wagon scout along the way. But their journey takes a life-changing turn when Rose is kidnapped by Indians. Daniel comes to her rescue, but the effects mean their lives will be forever intertwined.

Daniel prides himself on his self-control—inner and outer—but can't seem to get a handle on either when Rose is near. Now his life is bound to hers when the consequences of her rescue force them to marry. Now it's even more critical he maintain that self-control to keep her safe.

When tragedy strikes at the heart of their strained marriage, they leave for Daniel's home in the Blue Ridge Mountains. As they face the perils of the journey, Rose can't help but wonder why her new husband guards his heart so strongly. Why does he resist his obvious attraction for her? And what life awaits them at the end of love's winding road?

Printed in the USA
CPSIA information can be obtained
at www.ICGtesting.com
LVHW010250090924
790178LV00009B/112